The Oven House

Lynne Rees

For Diane
with best wishes
Lynne Rees
Mar'05

Published by bluechrome publishing 2004

2 4 6 8 10 9 7 5 3 1

First published in Great Britain in 2004 by
bluechrome publishing
An Imprint of KMS Ltd
PO Box 109,
Portishead, Bristol. BS20 7ZJ

www.bluechrome.co.uk

A CIP catalogue record for this book is available from the British Library.

ISBN   1-904781-33-0

Cover Art © Tony Crosse

This book was edited and prepared for print by
Associated Writing, Editing and Design Services

www.awed-services.com

...in certain lights, desire sprang up out of nowhere.

Barbara Gowdy
'Ninety-three Million Miles Away'
from *We So Seldom Look on Love*
Flamingo 1993

Our collective understanding of love is beguiled by love's first moments; and yet it is continuing, long-term love that we all want. Real love is love that lasts and withstands the difficulties which a prolonged relationship inevitably brings.

John Armstrong
Conditions of Love: The Philosophy of Intimacy
Penguin Press 2002

The Oven House

One

He leaves as night slips down from the hills. She holds onto him next to his car, her arms around his waist, face pressed to his shirt, knowing she'll have to let go soon.

'I must go,' he says, and his voice is a hoarse whisper above her head.

She opens the gate for him, but doesn't look up as he drives through, or as she walks it back and lets the spring-bolt clatter against the post. She doesn't want to remember this picture.

The gravel crunches under her feet. The car engine fades downhill. By the time she reaches the front door daylight has been swallowed and the cottage swallows her too.

'I can do this,' she says out loud to convince herself, but the shake in her voice frightens her. Again: 'I won't give in to this.' And she slows her breathing to control the tremble in her arms and shoulders, feels each long breath haul itself up from her hips like a climber who wonders if this last rock face is one too many.

She remembers the odd way he laughed when he arrived that morning, how he seemed too polite when he asked her if she wanted him to shave, and whether she had any wine, and she holds herself so tight she thinks she could break her own arms if she wanted to.

Shapes and shadows in the room merge into a wall of blackness as she sits on the sofa with a blanket around her. She's never been in a dark this dark – she can just make out the rise of her knees. She listens for sounds – her breath, the tick of her old travel clock, and outside, the river dropping over stones at the side of the cottage. If she went out she might see light – there might be a slice of moon or star to catch the bounce of water off her palm if she stretched out her hand into the spill. But she can't let herself move.

She doesn't know how long she sits there or what time it is when she pads blindly across the room to slip into the bed. The sheets are cool, and she smells him as she brings them up to her face. And strangely it is comforting – as if this slow-breathing dark convinces her he could still be there, or at the very least, be coming back.

When she wakes there's no sunlight cracking through the gaps in the curtain – the room is dark as if night doesn't want to go away but the clock says it's almost eight. Her arm outside the duvet feels cold. She makes herself get up, go and stand in the shower, presses her forehead to the cold tiles. The water comes from an underground spring and when she lets it run over her face the iron smell of it reminds her of blood, but the pressure feels good, as if the needling spray might be able to puncture the tiredness sitting behind her forehead and eyes. When she steps out her foot knocks against something. His bath-bag is on the floor by the sink. Her heart turns itself inside out. Maybe he had planned to stay. Maybe he meant all the things he'd previously said. Or maybe he'd just forgotten to pick it up after he shaved.

She weighs it in her hand then takes out the few items –

razor, shaving cream, toothbrush and toothpaste, a finger of amber cologne sloshing around in a gold-topped bottle. She opens the cologne, but the smell is unfamiliar without his skin to trigger the scent. What will she do with them? Maybe he'll come back and collect them. Hope trickles through her but she dams it up. Useless, useless. He will never come back. And she mustn't keep them, let herself be seduced into raking through them day after day, running her finger over the razor's edge, or dabbing the cologne against her wrists, her neck, making it all so much worse, if it could be worse than she feels right now.

She thinks of the days stretching ahead of her – rows of empty drums, but still carrying a trace of what they once held. She feels hollow like them, a cavern of echoes. She has to do something. She throws on jeans and a T-shirt, runs damp hands through her hair, grabs her car keys and bag. She has to get out of here. But outside everything reminds her of Matthew – the gravel churning under her tyres, the gate she has to open and drive through, then get out and lock behind her, even the sound of her own car changing gears on the hill – the same fucking road he took last night.

She needs to be somewhere he hasn't been, wouldn't have gone. Over the stone bridge and out of the village she takes a right, passing fields and fields of dumb sheep, then another right, onto the main road away from the hills, the wanting hammering away inside her.

'Stupid, stupid, stupid,' she shouts at the windscreen through a mist of tears. She puts the radio on so loud that the speakers vibrate and rattle in the sides of the doors.

In Newtown she finds a café, sits on the outside terrace, and orders coffee and a cheese scone. The waitress asks her if she'd like it heated up, if she'd like some pickle or salad served with it, and her politeness and smile threaten to overwhelm her. She can't take anyone being kind to her, she's too close to tears.

The sun is trying to break through the canopy of grey cloud, but the weather has turned colder today even though it's not quite the end of August. She rubs her bare arms but even this reminds her of him, how his palms moved slowly over her bare shoulders the second time they met. Just weeks ago. How can she be feeling so much after so little time?

She makes herself eat but it's an effort, her throat doesn't want to work, the food is sticking no matter how hard she tries to swallow. She can't stop thinking about yesterday, how he left, and tears drop from her eyes, clog in her throat with the half-chewed dough. She starts to cough and sob at the same time. The two women on the next table look over and then quickly look away, one of them fussing at a spill of tea on the tablecloth. She manages to swallow and clear her throat, wipes her eyes with the paper napkin. It seems so impossible to carry on with her life without seeing him, or talking to him, or even e-mailing him. But she has to; she doesn't have a choice. Though she can't see how she can go back home to David in a week's time either, acting as if everything is normal, as if Matthew had never existed, as if what she's done never happened.

She looks at her watch – nearly ten. David is probably making tea in their kitchen, spilling sugar grains over the counter as he piles in two spoonfuls. When he clears up he'll squirt in three times the amount of washing up liquid he needs for the few breakfast dishes, suds erupting over the edge of the sink. If he's working at home today he'll stop for lunch around one thirty, will read the supplements from the Sunday papers he never got round to looking at yesterday. What would Matthew be doing? She has no idea and she still wants to know so much – how he folds a newspaper, how he peels an orange, if he prefers to wake to sun or shadow, the exact measurement of his chest.

When she gets back she rearranges the furniture. Changing the pattern of the room might help – he was here for less than eight hours but his presence feels stronger than hers. She keeps seeing him stretched over the bed, his lopey stride from there to the fridge for the second bottle of wine, his chinos crumpled over the chair, his back walking out of the door.

She turns the bed against the other wall, under the slope of the roof so she can look out of the side window, moves the sofa to the wall opposite, settles her blue Indian cotton wrap over the table and arranges the fruit she bought on her way home in a china bowl. The two novels she plans to read she stacks on the floor by the side of her bed. She has to start again in this place. She opens the windows on both sides of the cottage. Fresh air rushes past her, and she can hear the soft scrape of low-hanging branches over the roof. She slides *Rock Anthem Classics* into the CD player and turns the volume up to ten, imagines the old tin mines that worm through the hills around her echoing with Deep Purple's *Strange Kind of Woman*. And she smiles for the first time. Hold this, she says to herself, keep hold of this.

She goes out to walk in the lanes, even though it doesn't stop raining all afternoon, and takes her hood down to let the rain saturate her scalp. She keeps walking upwards, always taking the lane that rises higher into the hills until she can't get any higher and the fields slope down into rain-fogged valleys on either side. She climbs up onto a gate and watches the sheep. When a Landrover passes the driver lifts his fingers from the steering wheel and nods in her direction, and it feels like a reminder that she can still be part of the world, and she waves back at him.

In the centre of the village she leans over the slate topped bridge and listens to the churn of the river. The day she'd arrived the water had been clear and still; now it's a stew of mud and rain and stones. Suddenly, from further down the bank, a heron rises from the long grass, a grey and ragged lift through the curtain of pelting rain, that for a moment lifts her, the heaviness dropping away from her for a second or two, and she takes her hands out of her pockets and claps the heron downstream.

That night there's a power cut just as she's about to watch a movie on the portable television. There's a snap and everything shuts down – the fridge rumbles, groans, and goes silent. The agency had warned her about the possibility of this. She blindly scrabbles for the candles in the drawer by the sink. The struck matches seem to hiss louder because of the dark. She leaves a candle alight in the bathroom, another stubbed into a spill of wax on the corner of the woodburner. She curls up on the bed in her clothes, searching for the scent of him on the edge of the duvet, but she can't find it. When she lies still and doesn't try, it seems to rise from somewhere, but so fragile that if she moves her head to breathe in more it disappears. Last night she'd sat in the dark after he left, and here she is again tonight – but one day further away from him now. Will each day feel different? She hopes so, maybe she can't expect better, but at least different. She clamps her palms between her legs, against the heat there. If he's gone why hasn't this terrible, aching desire gone too? Why does her body still pulse and moisten for him? Could this be all it was? Desire, lust? Was she just after a good fuck? Was he? Where is he now? Is he missing her? Is he even thinking of her? Fuck him, fuck him. But she still rubs herself through the layers of her skirt and underwear, and cries into the pillow as she comes.

When she opens the fridge in the morning there's a sour smell. The food she'd bought for the both of them stares back at her. She doesn't check to see what's gone off and what hasn't; she throws it all into a bin bag as quickly as she can – trays, packets, bunches of herbs – to stop herself identifying each ingredient for meals she'd so carefully planned. She allows herself to keep the wine, the crème fraiche, and the olives. And then before she can talk herself out of it she rushes into the bathroom and grabs his bath-bag from the floor and throws that in too. They're only things, dead things, they shouldn't hurt so much.

While she's kneeling on the floor and wiping out the fridge there's a knock on the door. She holds her breath when she looks out of the window and sees a florist van parked by the gate. They are beautiful – white and lilac flowers and some blue ones, shaped like bells, that she's never seen before – and she's tearing open the card before the delivery man has turned away and then she's crying again.

Surprise! I miss you already. Buy lots of good books.

Love, David xx

The card says, and she feels raw, like burnt skin, like nails broken below the quick, the breath in her throat as sharp as razors, though she has no right to feel any of these things, as she is the one burning and breaking and cutting up the life they have shared for ten years.

She walks down to the village to call him from the phone box. She'll thank him for the flowers, keep her voice calm, tell him that she's having a few days to relax and read before she starts her tour of bookshops.

'My mobile won't work here,' she explains, 'too many

hills.'

But as soon as he starts to talk, she bursts out crying, telling him she misses him, that she doesn't want to stay, she wants to come home, even though she knows she sounds ridiculous – she'd been so adamant about needing to get away, almost convincing herself with her arguments that this was a legitimate book buying trip.

'I feel so lonely,' she hears herself saying. God, she sounds pathetic.

He tries to make light of it, he even laughs and teases her, and she has an instantaneous rush of resentment for him, for not even trying to comfort her, and then she hates herself for wanting him to make her feel better.

'You'll be fine,' he eventually says. 'It's only another week and you've got plenty to do. Breeze? You still there?'

Breeze. His nickname for her. And the intimacy of it makes her want to cry again.

'Yes, I'm here,' she says. 'I love you.'

When she puts the phone down her hand is trembling, but she knows she didn't lie.

She finds she can fill the days – in the mornings sitting and reading on a rug outside the front door when the sun appears in weak bursts, or walking in the hills, and later driving to the towns she'd made a note of within a sixty or seventy mile radius and rummaging through their bookshops, sometimes buying a couple of volumes, other times a couple of boxes. She tries to make sure she's always doing things, things that take time – calling in at markets, local fishmongers and butchers rather than a one-stop shop at a supermarket. She has lunch in country pubs, or if she's close, in the vegetarian restaurant in Newtown where the bowls of homemade soup fill her up and slow her mind down.

One lunchtime, she's sitting at the same table as two men, and one of them turns his book towards her.

'Have you seen this?' he asks in a thick German accent.

The page is open to a picture of a cornfield, a shape like overlapping figures of eight cut into it. At first she thinks he means the book (she's sure she has a similar one in her own shop) but then she realises he wants to know if she's seen any of them in real life. She shakes her head and smiles a sorry, then turns the pages of precise patterns – spirals, interconnected circles, such wonderful geometry, made more wonderful by the overhead camera angles.

'They're beautiful, aren't they?' she says. So beautiful they make her want to believe in them.

When she leaves the restaurant she notices a little Internet Café opposite. She could e-mail him, tell him about her bookshop visits (the ones she knows he'd love or would make him laugh), the restaurant, about the men and the crop circle book. He'd e-mail back, maybe make some joke about her and extra-terrestrials. No. He wouldn't reply at all. It's over. Though she could check her messages. But she can't trust herself. She wants to talk, write to him so much, there is no way she could sit in front of a keyboard and not type in his name. She'll be crying in the street in a minute. Just go – walk, drive, do anything. Keep moving.

When the daylight leaks away she begins her routine of warming up the cottage. She lights candles along the deep window ledges – the flicker of them makes the curtains' blue gingham checks dance – and incense sticks she bought in Price's Candles Factory Outlet that smell of something woody and green. And she makes herself eat. But not raw, cold food. It has to be cooked and hot. She lights the rings on the narrow gas stove and warms a bottle of red at the side

– a 1996 Rioja or an estate bottled Shiraz. (She found a magnet sticker in a charity shop that said *Life's too short to drink bad wine* and bought it for David, but in the meantime she has it snapped to the metal frame of the kitchen window to remind her she doesn't have to be hard with herself. Not yet.) She poaches salmon, warms green pesto sauce with olive oil, and serves it on a bed of rocket, or she sautés slivers of chicken breast with rosemary and garlic, toasts slices of ciabatta under the grill. She sips the wine as she prepares her meals, the room lit by one lamp and the hand-dipped candles, listening to Miles Davis or Al Green or, when music isn't enough, she puts the TV on to quietly flicker and chatter away in the background.

After the second glass of wine her head and belly are warm, relaxed, and she is convinced she can get through this. He's gone and maybe it would have happened at some time in the future anyway. Maybe it would never have worked despite what they said to each other. There was too much heat too soon – it burnt itself out. Maybe it's better like this. And as long as she's doing something, and being kind to herself, perhaps the days won't scrape by so painfully.

She doesn't blow the candles out – she leaves them to burn down as she slips into bed, the cotton cool, a trace of him still there, or is it her imagination tricking her now? But it almost hurts, the press of the duvet against her shoulder, like weight, and like weightlessness too, until her own body heat starts to wrap around her.

But then the nights sneak up on her.

She falls asleep heavily for an hour or two, wakes with a start, staring into the darkness, her heart thumping inside her like a measure of loss. Mostly she lies there in the dark and makes herself think about him – the smell of him, the weight of him against her. She tries to make herself feel as bad as possible, remembering one good thing after another, the words he used, the promises he made – *your loveliness, intoxicating, you'll be safe with me* – and then adding one more to make it even worse. *This feels too important to walk away from* is guaranteed to make her body grind with the sheer waste of what she thought they had, what they could have had, and if she can still manage to bear this and get through the night, then she might be able to get through the rest.

One night when she wakes up from a dream of him holding her face, a dream that feels so real she can't bear the absence and the dark, she clicks on the lamp to read. There's a fluttering in the eaves. A large grey moth is hurling itself against the pitched ceiling. She tries to bring it down with the corner of a tea towel but it resists, moving further and further away from her. Then it starts to rain – dull and heavy drops that echo loudly off the slate roof.

'Fuck it fuck it fuck it,' she screams at the moth. 'Can't you see I'm trying to help you!' And she throws the tea towel across the room. She can't do this. She can't handle the hopelessness of it all – the ignorant rustle of the papery wings against the plaster, and these fucking tin-empty hills dotted with hardly used holiday homes, and the sound of the rain, and how it will try and fill the river at the side of the house only to be washed downstream.

But then the moth seems to understand what she's trying to do and it coasts down to land flat-winged on the wooden floor. She drapes the light cloth over it until morning.

At first light she scoops up the cloth loosely in her hands, carries it out through the door into the sun and shakes it over a patch of grass in the shade of some elder trees. The moth spins to the ground, lifeless. She should have braved the night, the rain. She should have stepped outside into the cold and not waited. She picks it up by the wings and drops it into the river, watches it disappear into the running water. There's a dusty charcoal smudge on her fingertips that she doesn't want to wash away.

Two

It started with one word. She was standing at the counter in Starbucks waiting for her café latte when she turned around and noticed the book in the hands of the man behind her.

It's the book she sees before she notices his face because he's tall – really tall. When she does look up at him she's conscious of how far back she has to tilt her head. And he's not great looking, his face is quite ordinary, his hair a nondescript brown, unfashionably long, and tucked behind his ears. But there's something about his eyes that brings a smile to her face.

'Marquez,' she says.

He doesn't say anything, just looks at his book and smiles, and it flusters her. She can feel the prickle of a blush around her neck.

'Your book, it's Marquez.'

'I know that,' he says. 'I just bought it.' His smile seems too knowing. 'I was waiting to see what else you were going to say.'

The trouble is she wasn't going to say anything else, or she didn't have anything planned. That was the trouble with her and words – she was drawn to them. Not just books, though she'd always loved reading, but signs, people's carrier bags, cereal packets, the label on the back of the toilet cleaner in the bathroom – *In case of swallowing…* If she was somewhere and still, and there were words around, she read them, sometimes aloud.

'Have you read him?' he prompts her.

'No, but I feel I should and that always puts me off.'

He laughs then, a big laugh that seems to come from a deep place, much deeper than his throat or chest. She can feel it lifting her and triggering her own laughter.

'I know what you mean. Do you want to sit down?' He nods to their waiting coffees and then to a table nearby.

She doesn't know why she feels so self-conscious walking ahead of him but it increases when she sits down, as if she could be sitting in a spotlight in front of an audience. Don't be so stupid, no one is looking at her, at them. And even if they were? What is the matter with her? Okay, she's having coffee with someone she's only just met, but they're in a public place. There's no reason for her to feel uneasy. But at the same time she's irrationally happy to be sitting here with him. But why shouldn't she be happy - she *is* happy, very happy, with her life, her work, so what's wrong with still feeling that in the company of a stranger? It's not as if she's planning to have an affair or anything. God, why does that even enter her head? And she can't understand why her heart is making such a racket, as if it could be drumming against her ribs.

She's rambling too, her words spilling over one another as she tries to find the right ones to describe herself to him. How in the last fifteen years her life has changed so much – she's moved from working in a dealing room in the city to running the reception for a local health club, and even spent one terrible weekend helping to train people sell showers in a Co-op in the middle of a rundown housing estate.

'Have you ever seen one of those wildlife programmes where a deer is cornered by a lion or a tiger? That's what it was like with the more aggressive trainees tracking innocent shoppers in the canned goods' aisle.'

He laughs his big laugh again.

And now she's running her own second-hand bookshop, has been for seven years and loves it, loves the customers, most of the other book-dealers, though some are a pain, always hassling for more than the ten per cent trade discount. But why is she talking like this to a man she's only known for ten minutes?

'Snap,' he says.

She lifts her hands in mock surprise. 'Don't tell me you've tried to sell showers in the Co-op too?'

'No,' he smiles back, 'I'm one of those book-dealers. How am I rating on your pain threshold?'

She blushes. Why is she such a blurter? But then there's a clatter from the next table as a teaspoon falls from a saucer onto the tiled floor. She turns and sees a couple, who don't look older than about nineteen, kissing and ignoring the fallen spoon. The boy's splayed fingers are pressed against the girl's collarbone, the base of his palm against her breast moving ever so slightly.

She doesn't mean to but she catches herself sighing as she looks back to her own table, and she's sure he notices because that knowing smile is back on his face.

'Matthew,' he says, and he holds his hand out over the table, palm up. She notices how long and sculpted his fingers are when they wrap around her hand.

She tells David about him when she gets home. A bookseller

who has a shop in Hastings, she got talking to him when she was queuing for a coffee. But she's aware that she's editing the conversation, there's not nearly as much laughter now, and she doesn't tell him about the kids kissing on the next table, which she's sure she would have done if it had been someone else she'd been sitting with rather than Matthew. She mentions that she might go down and have a look at his shop on her day off. Call in at some others too, maybe go up to Folkestone or down to Eastbourne, or Brighton if she has the time. She needs to do a book-run, she's got plenty of general stock, but she could do with some more art, some travel, some paperback literature.

'Maybe we can both take a trip down one Monday,' he suggests. 'Have lunch.'

'Yeah, okay.' But the scene in her head is all wrong now. The passenger seat of her car had been empty on the drive down the A21. When she entered the shop he'd looked up and smiled at her standing there. Alone.

This was so stupid. Of course she'd go with David. He loves browsing round bookshops as much as she does. And it will be great to have a day by the sea, find a good fish restaurant, spend some time together and chat. They should do that – they're both so busy, it will be good for them.

When she opens up the next day she checks the entries for Hastings in Sheppard's. If he's been trading for five years she's surprised he hasn't been to her bookshop before; most of the other dealers in the South East come round regularly – it's how a lot of them find their specialist stock, rummaging around in small town shops.

Matthew Pritchard Fine Books. The stock size is listed as 'medium' but she gulps at the price range – £20–£100,000'. Christ! She'd been gabbling on like an old hand and he had to be a major player in the antiquarian market. She hopes she didn't sound full of herself, but she can't help but talk about the shop with excitement and enthusiasm. She loves it as much now as the day she opened and sat looking in awe at the £10 note her first customer had given her, as if she couldn't believe that this was what happened – people came in and looked at the books she'd bought and cleaned and covered or polished and shelved, picked one up, and gave her money for it.

And so many people who come in the shop love it too – the smell of old books and dust and polish, beamed ceilings, Victorian fireplaces, the way she's arranged the sections in the different rooms, the hand-lettered signs, some order, but not too much, and the occasional cardboard box or old open suitcase with a scribbled notice of '3 for £5'.

Maybe it's not that surprising he hasn't been in – he doesn't sound like the Provincial Book Fair type, trying to pick up books from other dealers and marking them up by thirty per cent just to have enough interesting stock for their next fair. He probably does all his buying at the London auctions and sells on to private buyers in measured and hushed telephone conversations. She imagines him standing at the back at Bloomsbury, nodding his head or waving his catalogue surreptitiously, the gavel going down at four, five, six thousand. Probably more.

'Four second class stamps, please.'

She'd left the door open, so the bell hadn't sounded as the bearded man came in for his regular order.

'Morning,' she says brightly. 'That's 80p.' And she watches him fiddle in his plastic moneybag as he does every Tuesday morning of every week. She loves it all, the smallness and ordinariness of her village shop, the stamps, the paperback fiction, her bargain shelf, the set of old books in the window she reduces by £1 every day – an old Odhams set of Dickens or an encyclopaedia from the 1920s – that cause such interest to people passing by. Her own entry in Sheppard's is rather more modest – '£1–£250' – but it's enough for her. What she has is enough.

She's preparing a new Booksearch list when her e-mail bleeps. If it's a customer who's after an out of print title – good timing. But it's not.

> I hope you don't mind me e-mailing (courtesy of Sheppard's). But it was so good to meet you yesterday. And my book-buying trip had promised to be a complete waste of time until a woman in gold sandals spoke to me in a single word of Spanish. Why don't you come down and see the shop sometime – you might be able to pick up a few things. And I'll buy you lunch. Hope to hear from you soon. M.

She smiles at the thought of him checking her out in Sheppard's at the same time she was doing exactly the same thing, and e-mails back:

> Who are you kidding? As if I'm likely to find anything to buy in your shop. Why didn't you tell me you were one of the big boys? I'm just preparing a new Booksearch list – don't suppose you have an odd third volume reprint of Churchill's *History of the English Speaking People* (dust-wrapper optional) knocking about? Or any paperback Lobsang Rampas? No? Didn't think so somehow! It was good to meet you too.

She doesn't tell him that she is so pleased to hear from him she can't stop smiling, that she can't get the image of his hand holding hers out of her mind, or that she's already imagined herself walking into his shop.

She feels bouncy for the rest of the day. Doesn't get annoyed when 'The Anarchist' parks himself in the chair at the front of the shop and complains that people like him can't get work because he's over-qualified.

'I was called to the Bar, you know,' he says.

She does know because he's told her before, several times. She also knows through the local grapevine that he was a proof-reader for a publisher of legal books and was sacked for being disruptive and argumentative.

'It must be tough,' she nods supportively. And inwardly she smiles, realises that she wants to tell Matthew about him, tell him what happens in her days. And so much more.

She tries to check her e-mail as soon as she opens up on Wednesday but her damned server is down and she can't get online. She left home feeling uptight and now more knots gather in her stomach. She flicks on all the shop lights and goes into the kitchen to put the kettle on, leaning against the wall as she waits for it to boil.

She'd argued with David before they'd even got out of bed. One of those stupid arguments that seems to come out of nowhere but was probably due to her still being half asleep when he suggested having a barbecue on Sunday – they could ask Jon and Katie down, and a few friends they hadn't seen in a while.

'Couldn't we go out and have a pub lunch somewhere?' she'd mumbled sleepily, not wanting to think about people who needed feeding, not even David's son and his girlfriend. 'After five days in the shop I really won't feel like shopping and cooking for eight or ten people.'

'You won't have to do everything. And you know I always do the cooking.'

'Because it's not just about standing there basting and turning sausages and chicken breasts for half an hour.' She should have kept quiet. She knew she'd feel differently after thinking about it for a while, would begin to look forward to it. But she carried on, feeling particularly grumpy now. 'And you always say you'll help but then disappear into your office with a last-minute job, and I end up hurtling round on my own for hours trying to get everything ready.'

She should have kept quiet – it was too early for a row.

'You're such a bloody martyr.' David threw back the duvet, uncovering her as well, and grabbed his dressing gown from the chair. 'The bookshop's taken over your life. It always comes first these days.'

They'd just caught each other at a bad time – not enough sleep, or too much, or just busy thinking about other things. This wasn't a big deal – it wasn't anything. But it had control now.

'And you always choose times that suit you, not me. If you had an installation deadline you wouldn't be arranging anything for this weekend.'

She got up then and locked herself in the bathroom. 'Well it's your own fucking fault,' she said out loud but it made her feel mean. He'd been as enthusiastic as her about opening the shop, agreed to take the risk with her. But to be honest neither of them had anticipated how busy it would become.

In the months before she opened she'd needed him to go to the auctions with her. She'd been too nervous to bid, unsure of herself in this new world, hesitated over what to buy, and how much of it. She let David make the decisions, do the bidding. He just saw the fun and adventure of it, wasn't intimidated by auctioneers, pompous booksellers looking down their noses at a few boxes of paperback fiction or cookery books. She was glad he was there with her. But after the shop opened she began to find her confidence. David still told the same story to new people they met. 'I watched Breeze's knowledge of books grow at such a rate in the first few years,' he'd say. 'It was amazing. Ask her about a particular author, subject... she'll know something.' And he sounded so proud of her.

But it wasn't just that, learning about books – knowing what to buy for the shop or what might be a good private investment. It was the whole package – driving along motorways at six in the morning to catch the previews, bidding with confidence despite being one of only a few women in the auction rooms, visiting people at home and negotiating a price for their books, setting up a small business account with overdraft facilities, employing an accountant, installing a computer and software to run the business more efficiently.

Now she almost doesn't recognise the woman she was eight years ago. But looking in the mirror this morning she was staring right back at her – arguing with David makes her crumple so easily, feel so vulnerable, because it's so rare. And when it involves the bookshop it makes her wonder if he doesn't like the person she's become, and that makes her feel sad, and a little bit frightened, because it's a person she doesn't want to let go of. It's a person she likes a lot.

She makes a coffee and goes to see if her server is up yet, opening the doors of her 'Collectables' cupboard as she passes. She notices immediately. *The House at Pooh Corner.* Where is it? She's only had it a couple of weeks. Maybe it's been pushed to the back? But she has a dragging feeling that she's not going to find it even as she's pulling out all the other books. Fuck it! She runs through the people who were in yesterday – it was quiet, mostly regulars she thinks, a couple of people she hadn't seen before, and the stamp man didn't even walk past the desk. But she can't remember exactly. It has to be a stranger, not someone she knows, doesn't it? She feels sick thinking that someone who comes in and chats to her, telling her about their kids, or their holiday, or asking her advice on cleaning old leather books, could be stealing from her at the same time. She'll have to wait to tell David – he said he wouldn't be back from his meeting until two.

She opens her e-mail and feels instantly brighter when she sees a message from Matthew.

> One of the 'big boys'? I'll have to think about that. In the meantime, in an attempt to compete with your shower-selling experience, I thought I'd tell you about a job I once had in a drycleaner's when I was a student, as a result of which I'm now a whiz with a steam iron and dodgy chemicals, should you ever require such services. All of which is probably more information than you need on such short acquaintance.

> ps Thought you might like to know that I served the great British public honourably this morning, didn't let a smile even flicker across my face, when a woman came in and asked if I'd heard of Edgar Allan Poe, who, apparently, is the American equivalent of Shakespeare. Don't you just love 'em? Well I suspect you do much more than me. And I'm sure they must love you back – you have such a nice way about you.

She laughs out loud as she reads, and she catches herself smiling about his message every now and then through the day.

'You look happy,' a woman says as she shakes out a carrier bag for her books.

And she is, the crabbiness of the morning gone and replaced with something that feels like a balloon of fresh air buoying her up, even though the knowledge of the stolen book is chewing at the edges of her mind.

During a lull in the afternoon, she replies:

> You're right – mostly I do love them. But that's because we usually get such nice people in bookshops don't we? I have one customer, Big Ray, who comes in with his carer once a week to spend his allowance and every time he tells me, *I like it in here I do*. He is *so* sweet. (Why do they make him wear trousers that are too short and a belted raincoat so he looks like a Norman Wisdom stand-in?)
>
> Though this morning I'm not quite so enamoured – someone stole *The House at Pooh Corner* from my cupboard, and it has to be someone I know. Forget the £250 it's worth – how sick does someone have to be to steal Pooh? Unforgivable.
>
> By the way I'm reading Marquez's *One Hundred Years of Solitude* in your honour. Actually, not quite sure how that sounds! But I'll let you know how I get on. What were his stories like? Do you think we write or talk in e-mails? I think I talk. Have you ever had someone come into your shop and ask for a copy of *Lionel Richie and the Wardrobe*?

Her thoughts spill over the page. She writes much more than she'd intended but she wants to talk to him. She wants to make him laugh. She wants to be funny for him. And it seems so easy for both of them to be like that.

> I love the way we can talk so freely

...he tells her the next day...

It's rare to find someone to feel so comfortable with. Could we be soulmates?! I say that with more than a hint of irony as I'm a natural cynic when it comes to all things New Age, but meeting you... And you're right about Pooh. A hanging offence at least. Though I do make an exception for him – I don't have any time for the ridiculous prices dealers put on some children's books and if it had been a Rupert Annual I'd have seen it as entirely forgivable, part of a scheme to rid the earth of them!

Over the next few days she unpacks different parts of her life, unwrapping them and laying them out before him, e-mailing in reply to his morning messages and again to his afternoon ones before she closes at five.

He likes to climb mountains ('a sauntering kind of climbing rather than full-scale assaults'), has climbed most of the peaks in Snowdonia, is still collecting Monroes in Scotland. She likes mountains too but prefers them when they're next to the sea. He swims and runs in the gym. She runs in the lanes around her house and still carries a fear of water she's had since childhood, though it isn't as big and bossy as it used to be since she made herself take swimming lessons last year. His favourite novelists are Paul Auster and Richard Ford; favourite dead writer – Chekhov. Her favourites are always the ones she's currently reading – so it's Annie Proulx, and a stuffy Edwardian novel by EV Lucas called *Over Bemerton's*. She loves it for its half morocco binding with raised bands on the spine, the hand printed endpapers, and because someone loved this cheap edition so much they wanted to preserve it so beautifully. The content she's more equivocal about.

It's really dire at times but it can be quaint and charming

too. Does that make sense? I keep making notes of bits I like – *the art of life is to show your hand. There is no diplomacy like candour. You may lose by it now and then, but it will be a loss well gained if you do so. Nothing is so boring as having to keep up a deception.* Don't you just love it?

I love it...

he replies,

...I never want to miss the opportunity of telling someone how great they are. I have told you, in so many words, haven't I?

She finds herself telling him things she thought she'd forgotten (school, old boyfriends, her family, holidays) but that reveal themselves in bright flashes as she's writing to him. Then after she's sent them she worries that he'll think she's weird, gabbling on about her life to a relative stranger, and sends another one saying that she talks too much, that he must think she's completely mad. She imagines him laughing.

Do you have names for your customers? I have 'The Witches' who spend hours in the Folklore and New Age section (I bet you don't have one of those in your shop!) – one of them is about 5' 10", has a shock of red hair and is really intimidating. I have to force myself to keep eye contact and then I worry if that's the right thing to do! Then there's 'Colonel Blimp' who always asks at the door if it's okay for him to have a 'jolly old rumble'. He's wonderful. Oh and 'The Communist' (as opposed to 'The Anarchist') who wants us all to live on communes (obviously) and study at the London School of Economics. It's great doing what we do isn't it?

Your shop sounds wonderful ...

he e-mails back immediately

> ...and real – you sell books people want to hold and read. Most of mine will sit on someone's shelf and be adored at a distance. Tell me more.

So she does. She tells him about some of the customers who could possibly be the shoplifter. The woman who's been coming in for a few months and always asks for books that are in the back room – never art or history, topography or transport, always biography, astronomy, cookery, reference. Anthropology for god's sake. She doesn't seem the type to be interested in Levi Strauss's *The Raw and the Cooked*. But she shouldn't be so judgemental and it turned out she was after a copy of Desmond Morris's *People Watching*. Or maybe it's the two brothers who come in together, usually on a Saturday when it's busy, but occasionally on their own during the week. She thinks she's getting paranoid, suspecting nearly everyone, and wonders if the customers can tell by the way she looks at their bags or their coat pockets. She really doesn't want it to be anyone she knows, especially not one of the nice ones.

She doesn't tell him anything about David, doesn't mention him, but that's because the subject doesn't come up. She will tell him though. It's not a secret.

When she opens up on Saturday morning, there's nothing from him. She checks several times during the morning and is crushed with disappointment each time she reads *0 Messages*, then lifted momentarily when she sees *1*, flattened again when it's not from him, only some spam promising her 'Fresh Teen Girls' or 'Tax-Free Investments', and then annoyed with herself for reacting like that. Get a grip, she tells herself. She's known him less than a week. He has a life. She has a life. But she still e-mails him that evening before she leaves:

> I had a Summer Saturday Special in today – a man naked except for silky running shorts! When I asked him if he could wear his shirt in the shop, he said he wasn't staying anyway (some people just can't take criticism!) and his wife yelled at me – *Who the bloody hell do you think you are? Our money not good enough for you?* And I adopted a very stern (and worrying!) school-marm persona, called her 'Madam' and asked her to leave *my* shop immediately! Remember I said that *mostly* I love them? At least I didn't have to worry about him stealing anything – he couldn't have hidden a book of stamps in those shorts!
>
> So what do you do on Friday evenings (and Saturdays!) that prevents you from answering your e-mails?

She checks her e-mail at home the next day. She'd gone too far with that last remark. What he does or doesn't do is nothing to do with her. He's probably gone away for the weekend. Why should he tell her? But his reply is the first in her Inbox. It's timed at eleven thirty on Saturday night:

> Rather excited to receive an e-mail from you talking about nakedness! And also excited that you missed me. I missed you. I went up to London for an auction (Fine Art and Illustrated Books at Sotheby's) and didn't get back until late, and then every time I sat down to e-mail today some bloody customer came in. So inconsiderate aren't they? I've been meaning to say this and hope I don't freak you out, but I was very taken by your gold sandals last Monday, the way the bar slipped between your toes. You have great feet, and the curve of your instep is quite beautiful. Maybe I should stop there. But you must know

you are very lovely and very comfortable in your skin.

Very lovely and very comfortable in your skin. She can't get his words out of her head. They circle around, separating and regrouping in different ways. *Very lovely in your skin. Lovely and comfortable. Very, very lovely. In your skin.* She flushes as she scrolls up and down and reads the words again and again. They return to her during the day as she works in the garden, repeating themselves to the rhythm of her hands loosening earth around the new shoots of gladioli, when she stands and stretches her back, they stretch with her. And again while she's cooking dinner that evening, and even over dinner until she hears David saying 'Where are you? Did you hear what I just said?' And she apologises.

'Sorry, I was just thinking…'

'About the bookshop. I know.' And he sighs.

'No, listen, I forgot to tell you about this guy who came in yesterday wearing only running shorts…' She tells him the story, but it feels effortful and insincere. When he laughs as if he's really enjoying it, she feels worse. It was only a half lie – she was thinking about the shop, in a way – but it feels like a fish-hook in her stomach. Then she tells him about the missing book – she really has meant to tell him about this and can't believe that she forgot to mention it on the day it happened. She always tells him everything.

'You're going to have to watch people more carefully, not just the customers you remember being in that day, but everyone else too.' He leans forward with his hands flat on the table. She knows his mind is trying to work through options, come up with a solution. 'We could put some fake security cameras in – one of my clients has them in his antique shop. They look like the real thing – a red sensor light flashes but there's no recording equipment inside. It might put them off.'

'It feels so horrible that it might be someone I know, one of those Tuesday people,' she says. 'And one of them came in today – the dark-haired woman who works part-time in the dress agency? She had some books she wanted me to buy. Would a shoplifter do that?'

'If they're nicking stuff from other bookshops too, then yes.'

'Oh god,' she says and presses her palms against her eyes.

'Don't worry Breeze, we'll sort it out.' He stretches across and rubs one of her shoulders. 'We're a team.'

He's right. They'll sort it out together. So why doesn't she feel more pleased to hear him say it?

On Monday she goes into the shop even though it's her day off. She's always loved it more when it's closed and she can leave the lights off and wander round the silent, sweet and musty shelves alone. She sits at her desk in the semi-dark. She's been composing a reply in her head for the past twenty-four hours:

> Beautiful instep? Very lovely in my skin? Hmm… But thank you. Though I'm not sure about 'comfortable' right now. And you're right, the shoes are great.

And before she can think too much about it and change her mind she adds –

> How about lunch on 29th?

As soon as she lifts her finger from the 'Send' button she feels the weight of something, the physical ache of it, lying on her shoulders. She shouldn't have sent it. But it's only lunch. And it still might not happen. But it's not just that, the wondering if she's put something dangerous in motion here, it's knowing she has to wait for his reply. What if he doesn't get the message until later? What if he's in London again and she'll still be wondering what he's going to say tomorrow?

She goes into the back room and straightens up the shelves. Someone, she knows it has to be a kid because she's caught them at it lots of times, has pushed three shelves of biographies back against the wall. She slips her hand behind a few at a time and slides them forward to the edge of the shelf. Why doesn't anyone want to buy Gilbert White's *Letters from Selborne?* She's only priced them at £15 for the two volumes but they must have been here for two years now. They're a late reprint but still they're such pretty books with their title and a vignette in gilt on the green cloth boards. And the bevelled edges make them so lovely to hold too. Matthew probably wouldn't have them in his shop – too common, their covers rubbed by years of handling, the cloth fraying a little on the heads and tails of the spines. Even the shoplifter probably wouldn't want these.

Her hands are tingling. She puts the books down and stares out of the window at the backs of the garages. She can hear something that sounds like a welding gun or a cutting torch – something being sealed together or taken apart. This is wrong. Why is she doing this? In the ten years she's been with David she's never been interested in anyone else. The occasional fizz when she met an attractive man at a party, but even then she only had to look across the room to where David would be talking animatedly to a group of people, and she'd find herself smiling at how happy she felt knowing they were so together even when they were physically apart. But Matthew... she wants to see him so much it scares her. Her e-mail bleeps:

It's a date! I can't wait to see you. I only hope you're not going to look at me and say 'what was all that about?' I know I won't. I haven't mentioned this before but I can't stop thinking about the inside of your wrist, how cool it was when I held your hand, how I could feel the beat of your pulse under my fingertips. M x

His words tighten around her like Clingfilm. It's what she wants to hear, what she doesn't want to hear. It's becoming more complicated. She closes down the computer and locks up the shop, her chest tight with fear and excitement.

That night she and David go the local wine bar. They share a bottle of Shiraz; she orders the Spanish Charcuterie as she usually does – spicy *chorizo*, *Jamon Serrano*, sweet cheese, a slice of quince jelly and hot peppers – but nothing is right. The portions are small, the ham too dry, there's a lipstick stain on her glass. David hasn't stopped talking about some damned website and she wishes he'd had a shave. She'd told him to when he came in late.

'It's only Oscar's,' he said. 'Who do you think we're going to see?'

And he's right, but every time she looks at him she can't help thinking he couldn't be bothered to make the effort for her. But then all the little niggly things that feel wrong to-night shouldn't be bothering her the way they are. Normally she'd deal with them, tell Emma behind the bar. They'd be put right. But she doesn't want to. She wants it to be wrong. And if there's something wrong then she has a reason to be unhappy, doesn't she?

Oh-oh. Did I go too far? I can't say I didn't mean it – I do – but I'll do this any way you want to. I can do slow. I can do shutting up.

She keeps re-reading it. She should have got back to him by now. There's no reason why she shouldn't meet up with him and keep in touch. As a friend. They seem to have so much in common. And it isn't often you meet people in your life that you connect with so easily. They could be just friends. She just has to be honest with him about her situation.

It's hotter today. She has the door open and the sun slashes into the shop, heating up the books on the front shelves, and the few cardboard boxes stacked beside her desk. She can smell warm paper, cloth, dust and polish. The old glass that's still in the wide front window looks wavier in the sunlight – when she looks through it to the opposite side of the street, the newsagents seems to be quivering like a mirage in a desert. She leans back in her chair and closes her eyes, half expecting it not to be there when she opens them again, then gets up from behind her desk, stepping over the boxes, to stand at the door. The High Street is busy – people striding in and out of Tesco's, cars hovering for parking spaces – but she's only had two customers so far today. Though it's always quiet on hot days – book lovers, for some reason, are usually garden lovers – so she should get on with pricing and cleaning the books she's bought this week. She goes and sits back down and connects to the internet. She's acting like a kid. Just do it, just say what you really think.:

> I'm sorry, I didn't mean to keep you waiting. To be honest (here goes) I'm aware of being playfully flirty with you, and I do want to keep in touch, and meet up, but I am in a pretty long-term relationship. Ten years long.

And then she blurts –

I've now deleted about six different sentences because I'm stuck as to what to say next. Maybe I'm getting all this wrong.

After she sends it she reads through her copy – it sounds so naïve. What will he think of her?

Later, when the window cleaner is standing there writing out her receipt and complaining about how long it takes to get through the Manor House at the end of town, she hears a message come in and she thinks if she doesn't check it soon she'll burst.

'Mind you, shouldn't complain,' he keeps on, 'good window-cleaning weather.'

She stands up and piles books into her arms, books she's only just put there to price, and starts edging further away, and he eventually gets the message and tucks his receipts in his back pocket and leaves. She dumps the books back on the floor but just as she's stepping round the desk, one of the brothers comes in.

She wonders if the panic shows on her face, whether her smile looks forced. Her first thought is to phone David. 'Hi,' she says. Her voice sounds higher than usual.

'Hello.' He smiles and walks past her, heading towards the rear of the shop. She picks up the pile of books again – they don't belong out there, but he won't know that – and follows him into the back room.

'Where's your brother today?' She stacks them on the floor and then starts to tidy the cookery books, inwardly wincing at how false she thinks she sounds.

'He's working,' he says, 'but he told me he saw a new French phrasebook when he was in last week.'

'Just there,' she says, pointing to the top shelf. 'New-ish

anyway.'

He checks the price inside the front cover. 'Great,' he says, 'we're going on a daytrip to Calais next weekend.' He hands her three one-pound coins. 'That's right isn't it?'

She walks to the front of the shop with him. 'Have a good time,' she says. 'Bon voyage.'

He pauses then says, 'Mercy boocoo – that's the limit of our French so you can see why we need this. Thanks.' And he's gone.

It can't be him, can it? What about his brother? Maybe he's not working, just too nervous to come in after stealing that book.

Her e-mail…

Her hand trembles when she clicks on the message title: *Honesty* it says.

> Thank you for being so honest. I shouldn't have pushed like that. And you're not getting anything wrong – I scarcely know you but it feels like we have a real connection. I know you're in a long-term relationship – me too – but hopefully we can still get to know each other better. And on your terms. So is lunch still on? xx

At least they both know what their situations are now, that makes it easier, and they'll both respect that. On her terms. She can do this. And she has to meet him, she can't turn away from this now and then keep wondering what might have happened. And probably nothing will. She's making more of this than it is. She's only known him for just over a week. And she loves David, there's nothing really wrong between them, she's not looking for any way out of her life.

Three

She only discovered the bookshop because she made herself walk down to the granite clock at the end of the street, made herself move when all she felt like doing was driving back to the cottage and crying.

But she's promised herself she'll keep on with why she's supposed to be here; at least then she'll have some truth to go home to David with. The shop on the main street she's just spent a frustrating half hour in was mostly remaindered stock and bargain coffee table books, and the sixty mile drive's beginning to look like a waste of time, so she's pleased to find another one. It isn't listed in Sheppard's. Maybe it's new. There's a small sandwich board on the pavement – *Bookwise* – with an arrow pointing down a side alley.

She likes the shop as soon as she goes in and hears a bell tinkle above her head. It reminds her of the bell she has above her door, and the Victorian desk bell she puts out in the summertime when she leaves the door open, that needs a firm tap with a palm to make it clang properly to summon her from the back room, or the kitchen. The PC and software and the internet might make her business more efficient but the bells and the odd bits of book and writing ephemera she keeps on display in the window – a treen sand-shaker, old glass paperweights, some bone handled dip-pens, old wooden bookends – anchor her to the real world of words and books.

'Hello,' she says as she closes the door.

A plump woman of about sixty with short grey hair and wearing a baggy bright pink T-shirt looks up from what she's reading and smiles.

'I'm a dealer – do you mind if I have a look round?'

'Help yourself,' she says, waving an arm around. 'Would you like a cup of tea?'

She's so open and friendly it takes her by surprise. She's been used to indifference, or lukewarm responses in the dozen other shops she's visited so far. Though in a way she hasn't minded. She hasn't been sure, even after a week, if she could rely on herself not to burst into tears if anyone was too welcoming. And being left alone to sit on floors, to rifle through boxes and shelves has suited her. But today, this feels good.

'Thanks,' she smiles back. 'That'd be lovely. Milk, no sugar.'

The woman goes out through a door in the corner of the room. There's a clatter of a kettle, a tap running.

She scans the shelves in front of her – *Topography*. It still amazes her how she can do this – let her eyes glance across a shelf of fifty books and land on the one she's interested in, or drop down to the next and begin again.

Great – a couple of copies of Arthur Mee's county books. On the next *A Boy in Kent*, without its dust-wrapper but she has a customer who only wants a reading copy and at £4.00 she can pass it on at a reasonable price.

'Oh good, you've found some already.' The owner comes through and hands her a mug of tea. 'I'll get you a box.' And she goes out to the back again.

She can't believe the rush of happiness through her. A feeling of lightness that's so at odds with the shadowy sadness of the days she's been alone. And all because someone she doesn't know is being ordinary and helpful. She wants to hug her. She can feel the smile on her lips spreading to her eyes and she lets out a deep breath of relief.

'Here you are.' The woman comes back with a box that once held Italian wine. 'I drank the wine though.' And they both laugh.

She finds a couple more books and stacks them in the box at the side of the desk.

'I'll take a look upstairs,' she says to the woman who's looking through an auction catalogue, circling the occasional number, and only lifts a hand in acknowledgement.

She takes the narrow stairs two at a time, past handwritten signs on the wall – *History, Biographies, Travel.*

'Oh sorry… you made me jump.' She didn't expect to see anyone as she turned the corner at the top, but the man doesn't even look up from the open book in his hands, or step in closer to the bookshelf to let her get by. She squeezes past him and looks around for Churchill's *History of the Second World War.* Not that she wants to buy them, but ever since *Driff's Guide* accused her of charging too much for one of the most common sets in second-hand bookshops, she checks out any others she sees. £40 is pencilled on the free endpaper. Five pounds less than the set she's got at the moment but her dust-wrappers are in much better condition and in protective covers. She slips the first volume back into place, feeling vindicated. Then out of the corner of her eye she notices the man close the book he was reading, put it in one of his coat pockets and walk downstairs. She glances around – no security cameras. Shit! But by the time she negotiates the corners on the narrow stairs he's slamming the shop door behind him.

'That guy...'

'It's okay, I know what you're going to say,' the woman interrupts her. 'He's a local chap. Sad really – schizophrenic, comes in every week or so and does the same thing, and then his wife returns whatever he's taken the next morning, full of apologies. I suppose I should ban him, but... I don't know.' She shrugs her shoulders. 'But thanks for bothering, most people don't. And I expect some might even think about having a go themselves.'

She hasn't thought about her own shoplifter since she left home and wonders if he, or she, has tried to call in while she's been away. She hopes they made a special trip, that it really bugged them the shop was closed, that it messed up their whole day. 'I've got someone stealing books at the moment, and it's probably a regular customer, but I can't work out who. I just hate the not knowing.' She gestures towards the door. 'What if he takes something valuable and his wife doesn't bring it back?'

'Then I'll be full of regret and cheesed off with myself for being so naïve. But I'd rather take the risk. I don't know about you but I don't want to end up running a shop that has a list of banned customers or notices up on the walls saying people will be prosecuted for doing this or aren't allowed to do that.'

'I know what you mean – *No eating. Shirts must be worn.* I hate all that, but then again...' She tells her the story of the Saturday Special, and then carries on about her shoplifter.

'I say that someone's stealing but it's only *The House at*

Pooh Corner that I know has been stolen for definite, though now I'm wondering about a few other books too. It started a couple of weeks before I came away,' she tells her, but the memory of how things had been between her and Matthew then, how there'd only been everything to look forward to and nothing to cry about, seeps through her and her voice breaks at the end of the sentence. 'Oh god, I'm sorry, it's just…' she says, hunting in her bag for a tissue. 'It was a First Edition, and in a fine dust-wrapper. And I just wish they'd taken something else.' She's crying properly now and aware of how ridiculous she must sound.

But the woman doesn't look embarrassed or surprised, or suggest that a stolen book's not worth crying over. She steps around the desk. 'I think there's more than a stolen book going on here,' she says, and gives her a big hug, clamping her against her soft, ample chest. And that makes her cry even more.

'You must think I'm mad,' she says, after the sobs have subsided and she's sitting down on the other side of the desk blowing her nose and wiping her eyes.

The woman shakes her head. 'I did think you looked a bit fragile when you came in. You're not sleeping, are you?'

'I probably shouldn't be telling you all this…' she begins. But she does because for a week it's been filling her brain and she needs to hear it out loud to see if she can begin to make any sense of it, or if someone else can – how happy she was with David, the intensity of meeting Matthew, how she never expected anything like that could happen to her. And how could he suddenly back track on it all? After all he said.

'And I can't seem to get away from him,' she carries on. 'Even in bookshops, especially in bookshops, when I see something I think he might like, and I'm running through a whole conversation we could have, would have had, only a week ago. It's getting to a point that I can't tell the difference between what we've really said to each other and what I'm making up.'

'I wish I could tell you you'll feel better soon,' the woman says, 'but it sounds as if it's going to take you a good while to get over this.' Then more brightly, 'If you were my daughter I'd put you to bed with a hot water bottle, and make you sleep.'

She smiles. 'Thanks, and I'm sorry…'

'No need,' she says. 'And maybe it's not all as unforgivable as you imagine. You'll just have to go home and see what happens. It sounds to me as if you're going back to the right place.' She pats her hand. 'I'll make another cup of tea.'

Her head aches as she looks around the remaining shelves, as if all her thoughts are banging against her skull demanding resolutions. But she feels relief too – though it doesn't make sense that this one person, who doesn't even know her, can say that home with David is the right place to be, and can make her feel that she'll be able to find her way through this.

She chooses another half dozen books and as she leaves with her box tucked under her arm the woman tells her to call again if she needs someone to talk to, and squeezes her shoulder.

'Thank you,' she says. But by the time she gets back to the car she knows she won't. It's not the hundred-and-twenty mile round trip from the cottage, or that she's bought everything she wanted from there, or that she feels a fool for confiding in a complete stranger. She really does feel better for telling someone. It's that she's scared she won't feel that same welcome, that same spontaneous rush of happiness again. She'll open the door and the bell will tinkle and the woman will be there, smiling and offering to make her a cup of tea – everything the same, but different, because she was expecting it. Once something's happened it can never happen in exactly the same way again. And she'd be disappointed.

She's only eighteen miles from the coast and despite the gloomy clouds she decides to drive to the sea. Ever since she was a kid, and could hear the sound of waves breaking from her bedroom window, the sea, any sea, has been a place that comforts her. And when she catches her first glimpse as she takes a left hand bend, she's lifted by the stretch of it, even though it's an unwelcoming grey.

She buys herself a whippy ice cream with a chocolate flake from a van in the car park and walks along the promenade. It's started to rain – a light mist that she can feel seeping through her hair and onto her scalp. The car park was full but there's hardly anyone on the beach – a few determined holidaymakers wearing bright cagoules walking along the shore, a small gang of teenagers smoking inside a bus shelter, two elderly women leaning against the rails looking out at the water. She imagines all the other occupants of the cars tucked away in the cafés along the front, eating fish and burgers and chicken nuggets and chips behind steamed up windows, drinking mugs of tea, or feeding coins to the machines in the amusement arcades, or trundling around the craft centre she passed on the way here, or taking trips on the steam railway: all the attractions that probably pray for wet days and clouds to shift people indoors. But during the day, when she's not buying books, she wants to be outside no matter what the weather is doing. She needs to be in spaces that don't have edges to them, she needs to be able to keep moving, not walk around somewhere and come to the end of it and have to turn back. Even when she reaches the end of the promenade she can keep on walking along the road that winds up to the cliff, or step down onto the beach. And she's come here, to the sea, to do something in particular.

She walks down some concrete steps and across the soft sand to a cluster of rocks near the shore. She switches on her mobile. There's a good signal. She'll call David in a little while. She scrolls through the names until she reaches Matthew's: *Delete. OK. Press OK to confirm.* And she does, watches his name disappear from the screen. She does the same for his mobile number. The breath rushes out from her – she hadn't realised she'd been holding it in – and she looks out over the sea. It's almost the same grey as the sky, the surface corrugated, scarcely more than ripples near the shore, though she can see the swell rising further out.

'It's fourteen miles to the horizon,' David once told her, and even though she believes him she still can't make sense of it.

'Doesn't it depend on how close in the tide is?' she asked. 'How can it always be the same?'

'It's to do with the curve of the earth's surface,' he said. 'If you have a clear view that's how far you can see before it bends out of sight.'

She clicks through the phone's memory. *Home*, the screen says. But instead of calling it instantly, she decides to tap in the eleven digits of their phone number, slowly, deliberately.

'I'm sitting on a beach,' she says, 'looking at the earth's curve.'

He knows at once what she's talking about.

'Be careful,' he says. 'I'm too far away to save you if you fall off.' By the tone of his voice she guesses he's smiling.

'No you're not,' she says and he laughs. She means it but she feels bad as soon as the words leave her mouth, as if she could be playing a game with herself, trying to make herself feel better by being nice to him.

'What have you been up to?' he asks.

It sounds like an accusation, but she knows that it's only her own guilt colouring everything.

'Eating ice-cream, buying books, being pressed into large pink breasts.'

'Good, I'm glad you're making friends,' he laughs. 'I was worried about you being on your own.'

She winces.

'Drive carefully tomorrow,' he says. 'I'll be waiting for you.'

Before she switches off the phone she searches for 'Pritchard'. Then 'Matthew'. Nothing can come up, she knows that, but still a flicker of excitement runs through her as she presses in the letters of his name. How hopeless is this? How fucking hopeless is she?

Four

He named a pub not far from where they first met – it'd take them both about forty minutes to drive there.

She arrives before him and can't stop fidgeting, re-arranging herself on the sofa – sitting back, leaning forward to read the paper on the table, crossing her legs, uncrossing them. She has a glass of mineral water in front of her – she can't trust herself with wine, either to dull what is happening or to exaggerate it. She needs to feel as real as she possibly can.

He comes in carrying a notebook and a phone. He's wearing a blue cotton shirt. He smiles apologetically.

'I'm sorry I'm late. I got lost in the one way system.'

She stands up to kiss him on the cheek and he bends towards her so she doesn't have to stretch up to reach him. He smells of vanilla and something citrus.

She's flustered and she knows he can tell.

'It's warm isn't it?' A half smile plays around his mouth. 'Can I get you a drink?'

'Another water, thanks,' she says.

'Cheap date!'

And she can't stop herself from smiling back.

She watches him at the bar. He's taller than any other man in the room. At least six four or five but apart from that there's nothing distinctive about him. He's wearing heavy brown shoes, dark blue trousers. One hand rests on the bar as he waits for their drinks, the other in his pocket. She looks at his profile – and can't recognise anything familiar about him. She feels panicky. She doesn't know him. All those words exchanged but she doesn't know him. What's she doing here? She sits back on the sofa as he walks over.

'So,' he asks, 'is it a case of *what the hell was that all about?*' But he doesn't give her time to answer, carries on telling her how much he's been looking forward to seeing her again, and at some point he lifts his hand and begins to stroke her shoulder as he talks. And it's there instantly, the same rush of recognition she felt that first day. The effect of his touch spreads out under her skin. She's losing herself like she might under anaesthetic – if she counts backwards from one hundred she doesn't think she'll make it to ninety-seven. His other hand moves to her knee, then he makes a theatrical show of removing it and apologising.

'It's you,' he smiles. 'You make me want to touch you.'

Her shoulders tense one minute, then relax the next as she finds herself leaning towards him to listen to him more carefully, watch the way his lips move. And it's all so easy now, sitting here with him, talking effortlessly the same way they have been by e-mail for the past couple of weeks. She tells him about the mother who came in on Saturday and let her two year old sit and fiddle with the books in the Art section, his chubby little fingers teasing off bits of dust-wrapper.

'When I asked her to move him away she told me I shouldn't worry as he was very careful with books at home. Can you believe that? And I still don't have a clue who my mystery shoplifter is.'

'I can't stop thinking about you,' he says suddenly. 'Reading your e-mails makes my day. I'm so sorry I couldn't get back to you that time. I'd have hated it if it had been the other way around.'

It's so good to be sitting next to him, feeling his hand on her shoulder, catching the scent of his aftershave as he moves his head. But it's a madness, she knows that, he does too, how they can feel so drawn to each other in such a short time.

She picks at her lunch, can only manage to eat the salad and a few chips. She notices how he puts down his knife and fork between mouthfuls, so when he's talking to her, it feels like she has his full attention.

'I don't understand it,' she tells him. 'We hardly know each other. And I've told you, it's not as if I'm unhappy in my life. I've always felt guilty just thinking about someone else.'

'Do you feel guilty now?' he asks.

'Yes. And no.' Her head is pounding with opposites. She wants to be here. She doesn't want to hurt David. 'I don't know what to do with the way I feel. I don't even know what I feel.' She looks at him. His eyes are so shiny. 'What about you?'

'I have no idea either.' He shrugs his shoulders. 'But I'd like to find out. Wouldn't you?'

She rests her head against the sofa and looks up at the glossy ceiling. 'I don't know. I don't even know why I'm here.'

'But don't you find it exciting?'

'Yes, but I'm not sure that excitement is necessarily a good thing.' She gives a half smile. How is it possible to feel so happy and sad at once?

He walks her back to her car. She thought she'd understand more after seeing him, but she understands less. She has more facts about his life – about his wife (Hilary – she wanted to know her name), who's an accountant, and who he says he cares for very much, what good friends and companions they are; that like her, he has no children, never wanted them; that his favourite old movie is *In The Heat Of The Night*; that he's been to Japan and Australia; that he wakes up every morning thinking about her. And it all confuses her even further, as if each thing she learns about him only means she has to find out more and more, until there isn't anything else, and she knows him completely.

'I'd like to kiss you,' he says as they stand in the car park. He's smiling down at her. He places the backs of his fingers under her chin. 'Tell me how.'

No man has ever asked her this before. No man has ever wanted to know exactly what she likes before he's done anything. But she does know. She knows exactly how.

'Softly,' she says. 'No teeth crushed against my mouth. And moist, but not wet.' She begins to laugh – it sounds so organised and clinical. But he leans down and places his lips over hers. And they are so soft. He darts the tip of his tongue between her lips and over her teeth.

'Can I do that again?' he says so close to her face she can feel the pattern of the words against her skin.

She reads it again and again.

> You are intoxicating. And I am so glad you let me kiss you. Add your mouth to that list of beautiful body parts. But where do we go from here…

When she'd got home yesterday David was out and she was grateful for the time to settle herself in the house before he came in.

She was making a tomato and mozzarella salad when he hello-ed from the front door, as he always did, and the normality and familiarity of it sent her heart lurching towards her throat.

'Hi. Good day?' she asked, as he slid his laptop on to the kitchen table, then came over and flicked the kettle on. She carried on slicing the tomatoes, layering them between discs of cheese.

'Usual debacle for a company who thinks they want to upgrade their system, but have no idea of costs and timescale. But they'll probably give it to me, being the "techno-wizard" I am.' He stole a slice of tomato, then stood behind her and massaged her shoulders.

'Ouch.' She pulled away. She had no idea she was feeling that tense.

'Been lifting too many books again?' And he carried on, but more gently.

'Probably,' she said, thinking of the two tiny boxes she'd bought from a woman she'd arranged to see that day as a legitimate excuse to be away from home. Not that she needed one – David never questioned her about where she was going, how long she'd be. And a part of her had wanted to tell him the truth, because if she could have mentioned she was meeting Matthew – *you know that bookseller I had a coffee with the other week* – that might have diffused everything, might have made all the difference. She began to tear up basil leaves but then turned around and hugged him, holding her juice and herb covered fingers away from his back. She fitted so easily into his body, her head resting on the flat of his chest below his collarbone. 'I love you,' she said, squeezing him harder.

They spent the evening together, sitting in the garden as

the light faded, eating their salad with French bread and sharing a good bottle of Cabernet Sauvignon that David insisted on opening.

'So, what about our shoplifter?' he said at one point.

'I don't know. A few of those people have been back in and each time I sprang into action like an amateur detective in a very bad murder-mystery play – following them around the shop tidying up books and trying to look natural.' She was trying to make light of it, though David seemed to sense she was more bothered than she was letting on and put his hand on her head and ruffled her hair.

'And I found a hidden book when I dropped off the boxes today – it'd been tucked under one of the bottom shelves and it didn't even belong in that section, so there's no way it could have fallen and been pushed under accidentally.'

'You did leave it there, didn't you?'

'No, I put it back in the...'

'God, Breeze, you should have left it,' he interrupted her, 'then you could have checked for it every now and then. Narrow down the suspects.'

'Okay, don't have a go at me.' But he was right. Why hadn't she thought of that? 'I can put it back tomorrow. I just hate the thought of them getting away with anything else.'

'Come here.' He pulled her across the bench towards him. 'We'll get them. Don't worry.'

It'll be okay, she thought later as she carried the tray indoors, and David put the cushions away. Everything will be okay. Everything. This is our life and I belong here. It means so much to me.

But when she reads Matthew's e-mail this morning it's as if her real life stops existing again. For god's sake, she says to herself, you're acting like a school-kid. But no amount of sensible talking will stop the feeling of someone inside her begging to be let out, her heartbeat like a fist banging against a locked door, desperate to see what's on the other side.

> ...I loved touching you and stroking you. Please feel safe with me. Love – it's such a big word, but something to do with it is happening here, at some level. Thinking of you constantly. xxx

She can't stop thinking about him either – when she's writing out cheques for the end of month bills, or serving customers, or answering the phone. In the afternoon when she's alone in the back room of the shop, she leans against the wall and closes her eyes, remembers him kissing her, imagines his fingers resting on her collarbone, his palm pressing lightly against her breast. Yes, she can see him next week. Same time. But a different place – he gives her directions to a country pub she vaguely knows.

It's going so fast. They can't imagine not being a part of each other's lives, can only think about how they can go on together from here. Over the last week their e-mails have become more intimate, intense. When she's at home all she can think about is getting up the next morning and going to the shop so she can read his words and talk to him. One night when she couldn't sleep she crept downstairs at two in the morning to switch on the computer and log on because she couldn't bear waiting for another seven hours.

She asks him if he's ever thought of leaving his wife.

'If I'm honest, I have thought about it before, wondered what it would be like to be alone again, but usually after one of those ridiculous arguments everyone has, about not washing up, or something equally trivial. And it's always worn off very quickly. Now I think about being with you every day. But,' he confesses, 'I hate the idea of hurting her.'

'I've never thought about leaving David. I've always thought we were for life.'

She can't believe that she's even having this conversation. It's all so implausible – she's here with a man she's only kissed, a man she's known for a matter of weeks and only met three times, and they're talking about how they might start a life together. And David, the person she has confided everything in for ten years, is entirely unaware of it all. It's unreal but real at the same time.

He puts his arm around her and brushes his lips over her temple.

'You might find me completely impossible to live with,' he says.

'Probably,' she smiles at him, then stands up to go to the Ladies.

She looks at herself in the mirror above the washbasins. Her breathing is shallow, her chest tight, but her face is glowing, the skin smooth. She looks like she's dropped eight, ten years, that she's back in her thirties, before she even met David.

David. She can't think about telling him anything, not yet, even though they've had hypothetical conversations over the years about how they'd tell immediately if one of them ever met someone else, because they owed each other that much honesty. She can't even conjure up a picture of sitting opposite him and saying the words *I have something to tell you*, has no idea of how he'll react, what he might say. It's not something she's ever tried to imagine before. And it frightens her now when she pictures his face. She turns the water full on in the sink and opens her hands underneath the flow, letting it bounce off her fingers. How can she swing towards being so

sure about what she feels for Matthew, and then back to being terrified that she's going to lose David, the person she
has loved most in her life. But something's got to happen
now.

In the bar she's sure people are watching them – the
barman wiping glasses, the couple reading the menu on the
sofa opposite, a guy at the bar reading a paper. What she
feels, what he says he feels, the pulsing weight of it, can't be
contained between the two of them; it must be sparking
around the room. And now that they've been so honest with
each other, now that she knows how much he wants her, she
feels dangerous, a woman she hasn't ever been before. She
wants to slip her leg over his, lean forward and run her lips
over his ear, slide her hand along the crease in his trousers
where his thigh meets his groin. She can feel beads of perspi-
ration between her breasts, heat prickling the back of her
neck. She's drinking wine this week.

He takes her hand before she's finished her drink. 'Let's
go for a walk.'

He leads her down a quiet side lane just past the pub to
where his car is parked in a lay-by, under some trees. He
unlocks the door.

'Come and sit with me,' he says, helping her into the back
seat. She has to bend low to get in, the windows are tinted,
she can smell his aftershave.

'I couldn't bear not to be alone with you another minute,'
he says, kissing her, his tongue running over her lips, her
teeth. She lets her own tongue follow. He cups her breast in
his hand, circles her nipple with his thumb. He's whispering
now. 'I want to pleasure you. Will you let me do that?'

She leans back, and watches him lift her skirt up over her
hips. His hands slide around her thighs, parting them, over
the lace of her pants, pressing down, then sliding the fabric

to one side.

'Mmmm...' he says looking up at her.

She closes her eyes. There's a voice shouting in her head – she's an unfaithful bitch, she's in the back of a car with a man she hardly knows, in a public place, what the hell does she think she's doing? But her body is stronger.

His fingers move inside her and she moves with them, her breath escaping with a moan, her own hands reaching for him but he says 'No, let me enjoy you.' She doesn't care that people might pass. She wants this. This is the beginning of it all.

'Will you come?' His voice is urgent. He's kissing her eyes, her mouth, her neck. 'I want you to come for me.'

And she can't stop it now, the rush building in her then trembling through her hips and legs. He pushes his palm against her, and looks straight at her. 'I want to taste you now,' he says, 'and all the way home.' And desire floods through her.

If she closes her eyes she can still feel his long fingers inside her. Her hips shift involuntarily in the car seat as she drives home. Outside the house she checks her face in the mirror. She's sure she looks different. She remembers thinking the same when she was eighteen, the first time she'd had sex, convinced there'd be something about her eyes, her mouth, some sign that would give her away to her mother when she walked into the house.

Inside the door she hears David on the phone. 'Okay, give me an hour and I'll be with you.'

He comes out of his office clutching his laptop and a briefcase. 'Sorry,' he kisses her cheek. 'The system at Reed's crashed and it's their year-end this week. I'll be back as soon as I can.'

He stops at the door. 'You look pretty,' he says. 'I'll give you a ring when I finish. Maybe we can meet at The Hare for something to eat.'

She watches him get into the car and waves from the door, only yards away, but it feels like miles. Is this what adultery feels like – a great crater between you and your partner, the opposite edge indistinct, hazy, the bank you're standing on crumbling under your feet, and the drop so sheer and deep, you can't see the bottom? As his car pulls away she starts to tremble. Is this what she wants, an end to them? He won't tease her about her toes. She won't feel the weight of him curl into her as she falls asleep. But then she'll be with Matthew and they'll start building their own life together.

She'll be able to move away from the edge, soon.

She stops seeing herself – she sees Matthew seeing her. When she looks in the mirror, she imagines what he thinks about her hair – should she get it trimmed, keep it long? In Monsoon she tries on a violet halter neck evening dress. He'll like the way it exposes her shoulders, the drape of it over the small of her back, her hips. When she walks she walks for him. In the bookshop she moves slowly, aware of her muscles stretching, imagining how she'll stretch under his hands when they make love for the first time. The heatwave combined with the memory of him touching her makes her see everything in an erotic way – an apple core she nibbles the flesh from, the antenna on her mobile phone. When she's thinking about him her life seems hot and vivid. When she's at home with David, the colour drains, it becomes flat and grey.

She carries on e-mailing him, replying to his, but she needs to hear his voice now too and calls him whenever she can – from the shop whenever she has a few free minutes, or before she opens and after she locks up, or on her mobile from lay-bys on her way into work. He usually leaves his shop and calls her back on his mobile and she can hear traffic or seagulls in the background. Sometimes he sits in his car so he can be alone and talk to her. And he always sounds full of joy when he hears her voice. Yes, joy.

'I know it's an old-fashioned word,' she says, 'but that is what you sound like, how you make me feel.'

'Mmmmm…' She loves this soft sound he makes – a cross between a laugh and a hum. It reminds her of licking her lips after eating ice cream, or kissing underwater. He laughs his big laugh when she tells him that and it makes her feel like the tail of a kite bouncing through air. She loves his voice, its softness, the way he says *Hello you*, the way the words feel as if they're tiptoeing barefoot out of the phone and down the back of her neck.

'Tell me what you're wearing – I want to picture you.' He wants her to describe the colours, how the fabric would feel in his hand, how loose or close it lies against her skin, until her clothes touch her like the brush of his palms, his breath. She touches herself for him when they speak on the phone after she's closed the shop and switched off the lights, leaning against the wall in one of the dark sections, letting her fingers follow his whispered words, her own words slipping back down the telephone line to excite him.

'Taste me,' she says and listens to his breathlessness, can almost feel the heat of him. She feels so uninhibited with him – it's so easy, so deliciously easy.

But he wants to know about how she spends each day too – what's happened in the shop, funny stories about her customers, if she's bought any good books. She tells him about the book under the shelf and how she checks to see if it's there every day.

'Very Miss Marple,' he teases.

She tells him things she knows will make him smile. And talking to him, e-mailing him, she feels funny, desirable, exciting. And she becomes these things for him.

With David she's only what she knows she is, what he knows she is, not what she can be. But what about the good times, the great times they've had together? They're in her head, she can see them, but it's like looking at a film of another woman's life, the woman she's been until now and someone she can't identify with any longer. She can't feel the emotions attached to all those events – her body has stopped remembering them, how they made her smile and glow and feel so content. What is wrong with her? It's not that she wants to lose all those memories of fun and love and laughter she and David have shared. But this newness, this possibility of things between her and Matthew has silenced them; this newness is the only thing that makes her feel anything now.

She can't carry on like this. She's a useless liar, her face betrays her, and she can't keep on pretending, maintaining this division – this is the part of my life that I can show David, this is the part I must keep hidden. She can feel the boundary line pressing down on her like cheese wire threatening to cut her in two. It's such a huge relief when she's away from home, at the bookshop or anywhere else away from David. When she looks at him it's like looking in a mirror – all she sees is the woman she wants to be for Matthew and she's frightened that David might see her too. And she's aware she's acting, or trying to act as if everything's okay, except she's no good at it. Her voice is too animated, her actions exaggerated – the words and movements of someone desperate to keep a brave face. Except what she's doing isn't brave at all – it's cowardly and mean. One day she makes herself write this in her diary. *You are a liar. You are a cheat. You are cruel and selfish and hurting the person who loves you most. The person you still love.* And the words whip through her, but not enough for her to tell Matthew she can't see him anymore. She can feel herself drifting from David as if she's moving far out to sea and he's a speck on the shore looking in her direction. He's commented about her being 'in another world'. He's asked her more than a couple of times if she's all right, if there's anything wrong.

'I'm just tired,' she says.

He's trying to make light of it, she knows, but she saw the hurt in his face as she edged away from him on the sofa the other night, complaining of being warm, but really so alarmed at how aroused she was by thoughts of Matthew, and frightened that he might pick up on it and think she wanted to have sex.

It's been nearly three weeks since they last made love. Which isn't that unusual, they're both so busy, and they still cuddle up to go to sleep every night. But this time it's different – it coincides with when she first kissed Matthew.

Last night they watched a video together. There was an erotic scene towards the beginning – a naked woman caressed by two men, her breasts and buttocks soft in their palms, against their mouths. When David slipped an arm around her shoulder she flinched.

'What?' he said.

'You made me jump.' The excuse sounded pathetic even to her.

Later in bed he ran his hands up the back of her thighs and over her hips, nuzzling her neck at the place he knew she liked. It was ridiculous but she felt guilty about making love with her own husband. If she still did really love him as she kept on telling herself she did, then she should want to, shouldn't she? She closed her eyes, turned towards him and buried her face in his neck. When they were actually making love, their bodies effortlessly slipping into the familiar and comforting routine, she felt better. He was so gentle, his lips and fingers tracing the perimeter of her face. Maybe they should make sure they did this more often, put more time aside for each other. There was no reason for her to be looking anywhere else. And she did love him so much. When she came, so slowly she thought it would never stop, she began to cry and David wiped away her tears.

'You haven't done that in a while,' he smiled, starting to move inside her again, and she held him on top of her after he came, for as long as she could.

'We're okay, you know,' he said to her before he fell asleep.

She looked up at the ceiling, listening to the breath rippling in his throat for what seemed like hours. He was right. There was nothing wrong with them. That's why her attraction for Matthew didn't make sense. She should be thinking about not contacting him again. Stop it now. But when she thought of the weeks unspooling ahead of her she couldn't imagine them without Matthew in them, talking to him, reading his words again and again, his hands on her body. And as David slept she touched herself secretively and slowly, her thigh and stomach muscles tightening like springs, held back a gasp as her body sucked at her own fingers so greedily.

They needed to spend some time together soon, make a definite plan. She'd been away on book buying trips before. He must have, too. Then she could tell David, when it had all been decided. She looked at the rise of his shoulders, placed her palm flat against his back. So warm. Leaned closer and smelled his skin, the familiarity of it less like a memory, more like a constant presence in her life. What was she doing?

Five

He pulled into the drive of the cottage at 11.30.

She's been waiting for him since 10.00. He has the window open and she runs over and leans in and kisses him on the mouth, her tongue tracing the line of his lips. She hasn't been in contact with him for two days and it feels like a lifetime after speaking to him every day for six weeks.

He laughs. 'Let me get out of the car first.' It's a strange, impatient laugh she hasn't heard before. But he's been driving for hours and he's probably tired.

She's excited by her cottage, rented at the last minute and only from a picture. *A tiny cottage in a secluded setting* the brochure said. And it is tiny – its compactness surprised her when she first walked into it, it was even smaller than she imagined, but after being here for a couple of days she's grown to love it – the whitewashed walls, the wood-burner, old pine cupboard doors, the little hooded windows, and, one thing that had made her sigh out loud, how someone had loved the place enough to curve the skirting board around a bend in the wall, instead of making a hard angle, and filling the gap with plaster.

She'd explained to David that she needed to make an extended book trip, North Wales, the Midlands – she really had to refresh the stock, some of the sections were becoming stale, she'd visit a dozen or so shops, maybe a few local auctions too, over a week, ten days. She'd use the cottage as a base. And it was so quiet in August anyway – it wouldn't harm to close for a couple of weeks. He hadn't disagreed, but she didn't expect him too. He trusted her judgement.

'Maybe then the shoplifter will give up too,' she said too brightly.

'I thought you said it had to be a regular,' he said.

'It is... I'm sure...'

'You think they might move because you're going to close the shop for a couple of weeks' holiday?' He was smiling but it didn't sound like a joke.

'I didn't mean it like that,' she said.

He'd looked at her for longer than he needed to.

'I can make it for four or five days,' Matthew had told her when she'd called to tell him about the cottage. 'I guess we need at least that to convince us we want to spend the rest of our lives together. It'll be wonderful. Trust me.'

'It used to be the communal baking house for the village,' she tells him now, as they walk across the gravel drive, 'when there was a village here. It dates back to the 1800s.' But he doesn't respond to her excitement. He's waving a couple of flies away from his face, shaking a piece of gravel out of one of his shoes, then he has to duck to get in through the door.

'Well, I hope it's cheap,' he says, dropping his leather bag on the floor and glancing around the limits of the one room.

His words are like a slap.

But then he takes her by the shoulders, runs his hands down her back and kisses her so softly, lets his tongue slip back and forth over hers. But then he pulls away again, runs a hand over his face. 'Shall I shave?' It sounds overly polite. And in the next breath, 'Do you have any wine?'

She pushes away the nagging thoughts that he's not happy to be here. That's impossible; this is the beginning of the two of them.

She pours two glasses of white wine as he shaves in the tiny shower room.

'Do you mind if I talk to you while you do that?' She leans against the door frame and watches how he angles and shapes his face to the razor, rinses, and splashes cologne into his palms.

She is aroused just watching his hands move over his own face. She's sure that no one has ever made her feel like this. And why him? And why so much, such intensity? She can't arrive at any answers.

'I'm frightened my desire will overwhelm you,' he'd said.

And it has.

It's as if she has lost herself, that she's only a container for the desire that his desire has sparked in her. Sometimes it frightens her – that she's possessed by something she doesn't understand, that is stronger and more powerful than her. But she's sure that making love with him will relieve that intensity, that spending these days together will set them off on the right path together. So many things to think about, to arrange. But not yet.

She hands him his wine. He drains half the glass. He doesn't want to see the garden, or the river falling over slate and granite at the side of the cottage. He doesn't want anything to eat. Though he gives a soft laugh that sounds more like him now.

'Well… only you.'

He strokes her breasts, stomach, legs. He holds the arch of

her foot and slides her toes over his lips, sucking the little one before he lets it go again, and she gives an involuntary moan. He runs his hands back up to her hips and across her belly, lets his fingertips trace the lips of her cunt, before placing his mouth there, his tongue moving as if he might be painting her. She groans.

'Wait,' he whispers and turns her over, slides his thumb inside and presses gently like he might be testing ripe fruit.

And she does wait, holding herself back again and again, until she can't feel her head anymore and anything in the room that she looks at is fractured like the bottom of a kaleidoscope, until she can't contain it any longer and shudders and stretches out her feet and toes, her arms and wrists and fingers, as if the orgasm needs to surge out from other places too.

'You gave a little laugh when you came,' he says and buries his face between her breasts, breathes her in. She runs the soles of her feet up and down the backs of his legs. She can feel him hardening against her.

'You have a lovely body,' she tells him and gently pushes against his shoulders so she can slip from under him. She runs her hand over his skin, loves the way she can wipe away the sheen of sweat, then watch it reappear. She brushes her lips across his chest, his belly. He is so familiar, a body she has always known and has only been waiting to meet. Her tongue finds him like an eel, flickers over the rise and heat of him, the pulse in his balls. There is nothing he can do to resist her. He is hers completely.

She watches his face crease in pleasure, and her whole body shivers with the delight she brings him. So easy this being together, their bodies proving what their words have told them, that they know each other already, that now all they need is time.

They sit propped up on the pillows and argue playfully about which CD to put on – she feeds him cookies and he trickles wine on her; he won't let her get up and make anything to eat. His hands are constantly around her, stroking, caressing. She wants to open the windows – the sun is burning through the glass onto the cotton curtains – but he says no, let's keep it as hot as we can for now. She closes her eyes and tries to remember the patterns he is tracing on her skin.

When he enters her for the first time she tightens too quickly and winces slightly.

'Does that hurt?' His voice is concerned and he stops moving.

But she wants to hold him as closely as she can.

'Relax,' he says. 'It'll be okay.'

She wants to do this so much and his voice is the one she recognises from their phone calls. Soft, persuasive. And she does relax, falling into the wavelike rhythm he sets, feels him growing in her and then herself opening to take the full length of him. And it's his turn to gasp. They look at each other and she is sure there must be fear on her face too, because she can see it on his – his eyes startled. And she starts to cry and laugh to the rise and fall of their bodies, amazed at the power of it and scared at the weight building in her, the way he seems to be filling her, not just her cunt, but her whole body. The way that nothing matters but this – what they're making together that is taking and taking from them, and giving and giving at the same time, neither of them seeming to exist for it. He holds her hands above her head, stares at her.

'You have such a beautiful face,' he says.

When he comes it's like a tide, washing through her again and again, until he rests his head on her shoulder, his breath hot and fast and she wraps her legs tighter around his waist, pushes her hips closer and closer against his, feels herself trembling around him.

'Can we do it again?' she teases him within minutes, stroking the fine hair leading down from his navel.

'In a while.' There's something in his voice again. 'Do you have any more wine?'

He gets up and walks over to the fridge to open another bottle. She watches the plane of his back, his lean hips. She wants to touch him more. She wants to ask him questions, find out all she can about him. She wants to talk and laugh and walk and eat with him. And hadn't he said that in one of his e-mails too? *We'll do so much together. Talk and make love and walk. So many hours to ourselves… I think about you falling asleep in my arms.*

But he seems oddly quiet.

He sits up against the pillows and she leans against him listening for the beat of his heart. At one point he gets up, and slips his Chinos on, and she feels the colour drain from her face.

'I'm going to fetch a CD from the car,' he says.

When he returns and gets back into bed, his skin is cooler even though it's hot outside as well as inside; the sun is still baking the curtains and she can smell washing powder and dust.

'Why don't you let me make something to eat,' she says, leaning over him and kissing his lips. She thinks about the fridge-full of food she picked up in Safeway's yesterday, the meal she's planned for today – King Prawns with coconut and ginger and coriander, jasmine rice, *Medjool* dates stuffed with cream cheese and pecans. She splashed out on a bottle of *Pouilly Fuissé* too.

But he doesn't want to eat. Anything. And he doesn't like dates, never has, won't even try these.

His resistance to every suggestion she makes begins to irritate then scare her. She feels like a cabaret dying in front of an audience on her opening night. Nothing she says or does will bring him out of the silence that has settled on him. It's almost palpable – a grey mist around his head. And she can feel it – the hairs on her arms bristle. She's as physically close to him as she could ever get, but it's as if he isn't really there, as if the body she's touching has been drained of its life.

He keeps saying, 'Why don't you have a sleep?' But she doesn't want to go to sleep while he's awake next to her. She wants to stay awake with him, sleep with him. Why does he want her to sleep?

When she can't stand it any longer she makes herself ask the question. 'What's wrong?'

He doesn't reply at first, shrugs his shoulders.

She waits.

'I can't stay,' he says.

She can't believe she's hearing him properly, but remains where she is, her head on his chest, her own heart louder than his now. Don't say any more. Say you didn't mean it. But he carries on.

'The last couple of days, before I left... Things have changed a bit.' He lifts his hands away from her back and places them over his eyes. 'I thought I could do this. I thought us being together, being away from home... I can't do what we said.'

She says, 'No'. She is shouting but she can't look at him.

'I'm sorry, I'm sorry. I should have told you when I got here. But I thought it would work. But I can't... I can't hurt her.'

She sits up and wraps herself around the hill of her knees.

Her head might burst with the confusion of words that are banging about at the back of her skull, in her throat, behind her eyes. She holds herself tighter and tighter. Not once had she imagined the possibility of this. Afterwards maybe, a tiny niggling idea she's been ignoring, that when they'd both gone home something might have made one or both of them realise they couldn't go through with it all. Then at least they, she, would have had those days of lovemaking to keep. And now he was taking away that. Leaving her with nothing. Leaving her with less that she'd started with.

His voice sounds like it's coming from another room – muffled, a bad recording on someone's answer-phone. 'Believe me,' he's saying. 'Please believe me. I never wanted to hurt you.'

Why doesn't she want to hit him, punch him, kick him? But she wants him to stay, to change his mind, to realise the importance of what has happened between them. And they're here now, what's the point of leaving? Can't they still be together, walk and talk? They're still friends aren't they? Can't he see, feel, how good they are together? It wasn't just about sex was it?

'Of course it wasn't, it's not. I still feel the same about you.' He gets quieter as she gets louder.

When she realises it's pointless to keep on at him, that he will definitely not stay, she suggests they go out together and find him a hotel in town. At least they can have dinner together. He can allow her that at least, can't he? But no, he won't have this either. He has to leave. To leave here. To leave her. There's nothing left to beg for.

'Please don't cry,' he says, touching her head. 'Please.' But it's all she can do until he gets up to get dressed. Then she stumbles out of bed too and winds a cotton wrap around her, slips her feet into sandals.

'I'll get the gate for you.'

'You don't have to…'

'I want to,' she snaps. And she does. She can't lie in that same place as he walks out of the door. She needs to be doing something as he leaves.

Six

On the drive back home down the M1 she stops off at Watford Gap Service Station. It's the first completely sunny day with no rain since the day Matthew left but the sun doesn't lighten her mood – she feels mean and scratchy. In the toilets women are smoking in the locked cubicles. She stares at her reflection in the mirror to stop herself from glaring at anyone else. The stench of tobacco is so strong she can smell it on her hair when she comes out. What the fuck is wrong with them? Can't they even take a two-minute break for a piss without smoke choking up their lungs?

In the self-service restaurant she orders a cappuccino and sits in the almost empty non-smoking section – a corridor of tables and chairs overlooking the car park. On the other side of the smeared plate glass window crumpled looking people are shaking themselves out of cars, stretching their marbly arms and yawning, scratching and rubbing themselves. Fractious kids are grabbed and warned– *will you bloody stand still, you'll get the back of my hand if you don't…* And some older couples are opening deckchairs and thermos flasks and sitting next to their rear bumpers, breathing in the hanging fumes of their exhausts. The whole place feels like life is punishing her for what she's done. And she deserves it. Or maybe she's only noticing all the mean and ugly things because that's what she is – a mean liar, an ugly cheat. Then panic clamps her as she thinks about pulling into the drive and seeing David for the first time. And there's sadness and fear, for what she's lost, and for what she still has to lose, what she's broken.

She'd e-mailed a friend in Canada from the internet café in Newtown – she had to tell someone who knew her, but someone far enough away from her ordinary life who might be able to see things differently – told her she couldn't understand if she wasn't meant to have Matthew in her life, why was she allowed to feel so much for him. It was all such a waste – of emotion, of time, of love.

'Oh baby, it's like pouring champagne down a drain,' she wrote back. 'The loss of all those bubbles, the promises they held.' Yes, it was exactly like that. 'But, to be honest, if you were with him, if this had all worked out, I can imagine you talking to me, feeling this way about missing David. You have so much together. You have to believe that.'

She sips at her coffee and spits it out. Jesus Christ – long-life milk! She hates the taste. Now that is sad! Sitting in this crappy, smoky hole, comforting herself with a cappuccino made with fucking UHT milk! Behind the bars of her ribs her broken and ungrateful heart stops its grizzling and panicking just long enough to grin once. She will get through this. She has to stop looking back, going over it again and again. She loves David. She never stopped. And he loves her. That's enough. Please let it be enough.

He comes to the front door as she pulls into the drive, stands on the step and holds out his arms.

'You look lovely,' he says and wraps himself around her.

She feels so safe – raw and sorry and useless, but still safe. She relaxes against him, notices how his arms hold her but don't restrain her, not asking for anything, not expecting anything. Only giving. The heat from his chest warms her face, some hairs at the base of his throat tickle her.

'Something I said?' he jokes as he wipes a tear off her cheek. But he still holds her close. 'Welcome back.'

What does he think, what does he really wonder about all this – her strange moods, her jumpiness over the last weeks, her sudden decision to go on a book-buying trip?

He's lit the fire, has prawns ready to toss in garlic butter, French bread. There's a plate of tomato salad on the table.

He shakes a video box. 'I guessed you wouldn't feel like going out after that drive.'

He guessed right. He knows her so well, better sometimes than she knows herself.

After supper she leans against him on the sofa, watching the TV screen but not really seeing anything or following the story. She feels so tired, she could sleep for days. And for the first night she does sleep all the way through, waking to the sound of David placing a cup of tea on her bedside table.

'Good morning,' he says.

She's home. And the only thing she feels like doing is crying.

They sit outside and have coffee. It's rained overnight and the painted wooden tabletop is beaded with drops. She wipes her fingers along each slat and joins them all up. She's telling him about her walks in the hills, the day a sparrow-hawk flew from the trees at the side of the lane, right in front of her at shoulder height, so close she could see the air flurrying its creamy feathers, how she froze to the road to watch it glide up over the hedge and skim across the field.

'I know you're having a tough time right now,' he says when she stops. 'But we both know that we have a strong enough relationship to deal with it.'

She holds her breath, looks at him over the rim of her cup. She doesn't know why he's suddenly talking like this, doesn't know what he might say next.

'And I think it has something to do with the bookshop, how you've worked so hard at setting it all up and want it to do well. It's a big part of you and sometimes I forget that. And it's about us too – we're both so busy and we're hardly the earth movers we used to be.'

She looks at him to see if he's making a joke, to see if he wants her to smile, but his face is fixed, expressionless. He's staring straight ahead at the ivy-covered wall.

'Things change over ten years,' he says. 'They have to. And we could both go off and find other people if we wanted to, but we know that being with someone else wouldn't be any better. Not in the long run.' He still doesn't look at her. 'Different, but not better. We know what we have here, what we've built together.'

She's crying again.

'And I can't help you with this. You have to deal with this yourself.' Then he does turn towards her and presses his palm to the side of her face. 'But I have two things,' he says. 'Patience and trust.'

She sits there for a long time after the phone rings and he gets up to answer it, her head numb and heavy, her eyes aching. He's always been able to work out whatever's been bothering her over the years – worries, things that played on her mind – why shouldn't he have guessed what's been going on? Trust? He still wants to trust her. She doesn't deserve this. She doesn't deserve his kindness. But she's glad that she has it.

She can't stop thinking about Matthew. If she's at home she hides in the laundry room or locks herself in the upstairs bathroom to cry. In the mornings when she's in the shower and David's shaving at the sink, humming along to Classic FM, she places her hands flat against the tiles, the water running over the back of her head, and feels her body weaken under the crush of Matthew's absence, and the fear that she might never find her way back to David, how they were before.

At the bookshop she wipes the tears away from her eyes when she's tidying the shelves, blames the dust if a customer comes in and notices her blotchy face. Or she goes and stands at the kitchen sink and runs freezing water over her wrists, splashes it on her temples, breathes slowly. Opening her e-mails makes her feel sick, even though she knows there won't be anything from him, but her body refuses to be convinced of this, and her stomach lurches every day when she reads down the list of names in her Inbox.

Some days she's convinced Matthew was her 'enemy' – someone out to deliberately hurt her, determined to fuck up her life. She feels like this the morning after a dream in which she finds out he's screwing a waitress in a restaurant she is running. The girl is dark, her hair long and curly and wrapped in scarves, like a gypsy from a fairytale.

'Things were okay until I asked him to leave his wife,' the girl cried. 'I wish we could go back to how it all was before.'

And she's angry in her dream that she wasn't the 'only one', leaves the restaurant and runs home to find the locks broken off her back door, and sand and water everywhere from people who have come up from the beach and used her bathroom. There are traces of shit in the toilet bowl, dirty old rags left on the floor. She wakes up frightened. She was never the only one. There was always his wife.

Other dreams wake her in the middle of the night, her heart beating frantically. There are folders and files on the bedroom floor. They shouldn't be there. There are messages and letters in them. Who left them there? Did she? She dreams of a door frame dripping with blood. And in one she buys Matthew a book, but when she gives it to him he says, 'It doesn't have much depth, does it?' and hands it back.

'But I thought you'd like it anyway,' she pleads to his blank face.

Her Canadian friend had told her it could be years before she felt differently. If she really did love him she couldn't expect it to just drain away as quickly as it appeared. But she doesn't want to imagine time aching ahead of her and filled with missing him. The thought of days, weeks, she can just about deal with. But not months, let alone years. And at the same time there's a voice in her head that tells her she hasn't earned the right to feel like this – a grief just as if someone she loved has died. You didn't know him, it says. You only spent hours with him. You've made this all up. It's not real. But no matter how much she tries to change it all, how she agrees with the voice, makes herself focus on other things – preparing Booksearch lists every week instead of once a month, hauling boxes from one end of the shop to the other, driving out to people's houses to look at books even if they sound hopeless – the grief always returns, catching her un-awares, and she finds herself crying, for what seems like no reason, though the reason is sitting inside her – two rocks grinding away at each other.

She decides to move some of the sections around in the

shop, choosing two that are the furthest apart – Paperback Literature and Natural History – to make sure it'll take her all day and that by the end of it she'll be too tired to think of anything else.

She remembers the 'plant' when she's clearing out the large format books from the bottom shelf. It's been there every time she's checked over the last weeks and she's been thinking of putting it back in its right section. She's stopped caring so much, stopped worrying if people were stuffing books in their pockets or bags when they were alone in the back room. Maybe the shoplifter did give up because she was closed for those weeks in August. At least that would be some good to come out of her trip away. But her feeble attempt at irony doesn't make her smile.

She slips her hand underneath the shelf certain that she'll feel the spine. But it's not there. She lies down on the floor and peers into the two inches of darkness, running her hand along the length, and then under the shelf next to it, only finding a five pence piece and a sweet wrapper in the dust. Maybe it wasn't this shelf. But she knows it is. She only checked it the day before yesterday, just before she locked up. She scrambles up, turns the 'Back in Five Minutes' sign around and calls David.

'It has to be someone who was in yesterday,' she says. 'And it was pouring with rain for most of the day, there was hardly…' She mentally ticks off the customers. She can't remember more than about four.

'What about the brothers?' David asks.

'No. Mrs Banks came in from the school. Someone I've never seen before bought a pile of paperbacks to take away on holiday but didn't move from that section, I'm sure. Colonel Blimp was in for about half an hour. I hope it's not him.' She looks in the shop cash book – she'd written a sale down just before she closed at five thirty. 'And a guy came in just as I was going to close, so I stayed open a bit longer. I think I've mentioned him to you before, really chatty, used to be in the army. His wax coat was dripping all over the place. But he bought a book.' She presses her finger to the page. '£6.00. One of those Edwardian Lady flower books. He said it was a birthday present for his sister. You wouldn't spend six pounds on a book if you were there to steal one would you?'

She can tell by David's silence that that's exactly what he thinks someone might do.

'I can't remember him being in that first time. But maybe he was. He's been coming in the shop for ages, at least a year. Maybe longer.' She hates the plaintive tone in her voice. 'I've got to go,' she says. 'There's someone peering in at the window.' She's been closed for longer than five minutes.

'Let's decide what to do tonight,' David says. 'We can't be absolutely sure it's him at the moment.'

Her legs feel wobbly as she opens the door and apologises to the woman waiting outside.

She goes back to the Natural History section and checks under all the shelves again. If it is him then he's bloody good. He was chatting to her about his holiday in Spain, how he prefers the coastal resorts around Barcelona to the southern beaches. He'd been looking at properties for sale just inland he said. You could still pick up something that needed renovation for about £20,000. She and David had been to Barcelona the year before and she'd mentioned some of the places they'd visited, though he said he hadn't spent much time in the city. When she closed up he'd even offered to help her with the door. It had swollen up in the wet weather and he pulled it tight so she could lock it.

She feels like crying. If it is him he must have been thinking what a gullible fool she was.

She still has all Matthew's e-mails and reads through them. It all sounds so real, that he meant everything he said to her. Or was she blinkered to what was really happening? Was it all a stupid romantic illusion? Did she make it all up? But if she did, why can't she unmake it? Did she convince him it was all possible too — for a little while? It was her fault. She gave him too much of herself and now he's handed it all back she can't get it to fit again. And why? why? why? The word scores the inside of her head as it spins round and round. But she doesn't know the 'why', she only knows the 'what' of it all — what happened in the past and what she feels now, in the present. And when she tries to imagine any 'what' she and Matthew might have had together in the future, any real life, her mind narrows. She can't picture them doing things together — never at airports deciding on their duty free, or walking along a beach together, or moving furniture, or cooking. He never, in her imagination, has a problem and asks her what he should do. They're never in the bathroom together, getting in each other's way, or one of them shouting 'Don't forget to pick up some milk' as they close the front door. Ordinary things. No, the only thing she can see them doing is making love or telling each other about their lives before they met, their words spinning out and around each other, making a world of their own. A world where it always seems to be hot and sunny, just like the day they met and the weeks that followed. If she really tries hard, forces herself to make a picture, she can just about see them sitting around a table with some people she doesn't know, his friends maybe, but she's finding it so difficult to be part of it all, the conversation's too particular for her to enter. The light's good though. And she looks good. A woman who's desired, who desires – the woman she became under his gaze, his attention – always glows.

Even though Matthew fills her thoughts she feels closer to David. She doesn't have that constant, anxious fizzing in her body any more – how she felt waiting for Matthew's messages, the anticipation of speaking to him, the disappointment of not. She realises how much that spilled over into her life with David – how that division she created was a mountain she was making herself climb every day, exhausting her body and mind. And she doesn't know if it's just her, or whether David is being different too, but they don't bicker, they don't rush past each other on the way out to work, make abrupt phone calls from the supermarket to see if one of them can remember what they've run out of. They are kinder and slower. And she likes the pace of that.

He buys her yellow rosebuds. She rubs his back when she wakes in the morning, presses her face into his skin for his familiar smell. After having coffee together he's got into the habit of placing both his hands on her shoulders and kissing the top of her head. It makes her close her eyes, removes the weight from her heart for a time.

One evening they slouch on the sofa with their feet up on the footstool, sharing a bottle of wine and passing olives and Kettle crisps to each other, neither of them wanting to get up and put the light on, happy for the dark to slide around them. David is trying to think of ways to catch their suspected shoplifter.

'I feel so stupid,' she says. 'If he's been doing this regularly why haven't I noticed?'

'You've got nearly 20,000 books in that shop, Breeze. You can't remember them all. And if he has been lifting the odd book from the general stock and getting away with it, then maybe that's why he took a chance on a more valuable one.'

'*Secrets of Pistoulet,*' she says. 'That was the book under the shelf. It wasn't that valuable, a remainder I ordered off the Texas Bookman catalogue. But it was so lovely with a slipcase and decorative tissue pages, and full of recipes and stories for making people feel better.'

She nearly tells him.

It's suddenly too big for her to carry around on her own – she needs to let it out so they can both move forward from it. It feels like a wall between them – one she can see over but not get around. Her heart pounds, she goes cold, and her tongue starts to move with the words – *I've got something terrible to tell you.* If she opened her mouth she's sure they would fall out. But she doesn't. What good would it do? Make her feel better? Shouldn't she take responsibility for that, not turn to David for it? The words slip away from her tongue. She's always needed to speak about things in the past, get problems out in the open. But maybe that's not always the right thing to do. Some things might be better left unsaid, unwrapped, not allowed to jump into the light, eager to kick someone in the face. Hadn't he said he couldn't help her with this?

'I said a shoplifter with good taste then?' David jokes.

'Who likes cooking?' she joins in.

'That narrows it down – keep your eyes open for someone in a chef's hat.'

They start laughing, getting more and more ridiculous with their suggestions. 'And an apron with big pockets.'

She'd forgotten how good it felt, how easy it has always been for them to be silly together.

'My money's on the army guy though,' he says when they

stop laughing.

'Why?' she says.

He shrugs. 'Intuition. All those hidden pockets in a wax coat. And how chatty you say he is all the time. Most people in bookshops are quiet as they browse around. Sounds like he's saying too much, trying to distract you.'

She wants to object that she's not that naïve. But if he is the one stealing from her, then she is. And what about Matthew? How easily did she believe everything he had to say?

'If he comes in again, telephone me and ask... I don't know... *What's the time of the last post?* Pretend you're calling the Post Office. Or something like that, make up a question and I'll drive up straight away.'

'It makes me feel nervous,' she says. 'What if he suspects something? What if he gets angry?'

'Breeze, I'll be less than five minutes away. You're going to have to trust me on this, okay?'

'Okay,' she says. She wants it to be over.

At times her heart feels tight, cramped. She doesn't know if it's because she's not letting love in, or if she can't let it out. But something is stuck. Can you get indigestion of the heart? Stop it. She shouldn't make light of it. And she's making herself sound like a character from a sentimental TV show, all angst and self-indulgence. She's responsible for what she's feeling. She's the only one. Which means she's the only one who can get her out of it. And she has to be honest with herself – does she want to? Does she really want to let go of her desire for Matthew, the excitement it can still make her feel, and settle for what she has. Settle? It sounds second-best, what's left on the plate, giving up on what she really wants, giving in. It is not those things, it is others too – *settle: cease from wandering, disturbance; attain certainty, composure or quietness;*

remedy the disordered state. She closes the dictionary and holds it in both hands as if she could be making a promise on it before putting it back on the shelf. How far away from herself did she have to travel to begin to find her way back?

She hears the shop doorbell ring and walks back down to the front of the shop. Her suspected shoplifter is standing in front of the Railway books. She's sure she doesn't change her stride though inside she feels like she's walking on eggshells.

'Hi,' she says. Did that sound false? She can't trust her own judgement anymore.

'Hi. How's business?' he asks.

She can't believe his cheek. As it's been weeks since you've been in, business is fine, she feels like saying.

'Not bad,' she says. Maybe she and David are wrong. There'd been other people that day. Maybe it's someone so clever she's not suspecting them at all.

He wanders over to the Collectables cupboard. She put a first edition of Bleak House in there last Saturday. And a Helen Allingham book she's had at home for a few months. It's £150. She clenches her jaw. Damn him – money has never been her primary reason for running the shop, but since these thefts she finds herself thinking about it more and more, and she hates him for doing this to her. Innocent until proven guilty, her mind says, but her eyes are stretching to their corners to see what he's doing.

She should call David. She hopes he's there.

The guy stares at the books on the cupboard shelves for a few minutes and then moves away to the paperback fiction, picks up a Patricia Cornwell novel, reads the blurb, then replaces it. He squats down to look at the books stacked on the floor, and slides one out from the bottom of the pile.

'This'll do,' he says. 'Some easy reading.'

She normally doesn't pay too much attention to the paperbacks she sells, she has so many, but she can't help noticing everything about this one – John Grisham's *The Pelican Brief* with an old Waterstone's '3 for 2' yellow sticker still on the front. There's a telephone number scribbled in biro at the top of the first page where she's pencilled the price, £1.50. The spine has a few light creases down it.

He squeezes his hand into the pocket of his jeans for some change. It's then she realises he's only wearing a sweater. No jacket or coat. It's a nice day, one of those odd November days that feel more like September. She remembers what David said about the wax coat. He doesn't have any pockets. So is this what he does – comes in and looks around for what he wants, then comes back on another day, in his coat, maybe days or a week later, maybe on a Saturday, when there are more people in the shop and she's busy with other customers, searching through the shelves for them, or taking details of an out of print title?

'So have you decided about Spain?' she asks him when she hands him his fifty pence change.

'Not really,' he says. 'I'd like to go back in the New Year and see how I feel about the place out of season.'

'What's the temperature this time of year?' she prompts. She wants to hear him talk now, to listen hard and try and work out whether there's more between and behind his words. All she has to do is be more aware, not allow herself to be drawn in by what he's saying.

But he has to go. 'I'll pop back when I have more time,' he says and lifts the book in a goodbye wave.

She still can't be certain it's him but going on what she feels – excitement, fear, relief, a mix of them all – something isn't right. She calls David straight away.

She's sitting on the upstairs toilet with the bathroom door

open looking at the Victorian quilt hanging on the landing wall. 'It's an upright piano cover,' the dealer in the antique fair had told her. She didn't have a piano but she'd bought it because she loved the scrappy pieces of old velvet - browns, golds, moss greens, and reds with their pile worn and rubbed, some fading patches of brocade – all sewn together into an oblong. Suddenly she sees the woman – the triangle of skirt, a bell shaped top, the sphere of her head bobbing above the scoop of a neckline – and smiles at her discovery. Then she notices she has legs too, big cartoon trunks with clown feet shapes at the ends, and they're bent as if they're running underneath her. But her body just floats above them, as if she has no idea of their intention, of where they might be taking her. The door frame cuts off both edges of the quilt and she wonders if there's anything else she hasn't noticed before – something behind the jigsaw woman that could be chasing her, or a mysterious shape ahead of her that's attracting her attention. Something that has to be more interesting, more exciting than the familiar shapes she's used to having around her, day after day.

Why does she still want Matthew so much? Is it because she can't have him now? Was she ever shaken by so much desire before? She must have been. When she and David met they couldn't stop touching each other – they made love so often, spent whole weekends in bed, only leaving it to make something to eat but then clambering back in, balancing plates and glasses and cups – but she can't physically remember the intensity of that now. Maybe how she feels about Matthew will fade too. She hopes so, that the images of him stay in her memory, like a gallery of old photos, but the desire fades, stops flaming through her, making her compare her life, its comfort and safety, its nurturing and steady love, to that

92 – Lynne Rees

heat. But it's not just the idea and memory of making love with Matthew. She misses his voice, his words. The times in the day that she'd put aside to speak to him – she made him a part of her life so quickly, so intensely. She wants to shake him out of her and shake him deeper into her. She wishes she'd never met him, and is glad that she did. It felt so easy, so right. And so wrong. What else was she wrong about? That he was a lot like her. That he felt what she felt. This is what hurts and confuses her most, the thought that it might not have been real for him, that it was the chase, the fuck. That she was easily deceived. By him. By herself.

When she feels like this she makes herself run – she's learned that she can't cry and run at the same time, that she doesn't have to let her mind torture her and that she can use it to push and urge her body up the long slow hill that leads away from home. That by the time she's taken the double bend at the top she's grateful for the ache of her muscles. And then the flat stretch into the village, past the pub and the cricket pitch and then the open fields where she picks up speed and feels like she's running into a future.

The first few days she was home she'd wanted to make love to David so much. She slept leaning into his back, her leg draped over his. He'd sigh if she ran her hands over his shoulders, his waist, his hips. If they made love would that make all the difference? Would that rescue her? Wouldn't that begin to heal everything? But who would she be thinking of? She couldn't do that, not now. And maybe he did know something, because although he cuddled and stroked her, and sometimes held her so tight she had to joke *I can't breathe!*, he didn't press for sex. 'Patience and trust,' he'd said.

Everyone who comes in complains of the cold, the rain.

Their umbrellas drip in the clay pot behind the door, wet footprints trail them round the aisles. She wants to e-mail Matthew so much. But she mustn't get in touch. It would only drag her back to where she was a couple of months ago. She can't trust herself not to cry over him, tell him again and again what he walked away from, how badly he hurt her. But she also wants to know he's okay. And the bookshop reminds her so much of him – the connection they made at the very beginning. She writes to him in her head, measuring her words and phrases then deleting them over and over in an attempt to find the right thing to say. But there's no such thing as the right thing, she knows that.

There's a rush of cold air as one customer leaves. She reaches down behind her desk and turns up the thermostat on the radiator and there's another cold blast as the door opens again. Even though she's been expecting him she still feels her mouth go dry when he steps in, tugging at the swollen door to close it properly after him, making a show of shaking his hands and unzipping his wax coat, shiny with rain.

'God it's wet out there,' he says. 'What I wouldn't give to be in Spain now.'

'Do you want to take that off?' she asks. 'Leave it on the chair? I'll keep an eye on it.'

He looks at the chair next to her desk and then back at her. She hopes she has a natural smile on her face, though her cheeks feel stiff, as if it's been stapled there.

'No, I'll be okay,' he says. 'It's not that wet.'

She picks up the phone as he walks down the shop and into one of the aisles on the right. *Art and Architecture*. She hopes she can keep the shake out of her voice.

'Could you tell me the time of the last post today?' she says when David answers.

'Fucking hell,' he says. 'Is he there? I was just making something to eat.'

The guy walks out of the aisle and heads towards the back room.

'17.50? And that's from the main Post Office?' Just get here quick, she wants to shout. Forget about your fucking lunch! What if he's already stuffing books in his pockets and getting ready to leave? Why is she so certain that it is him?

She puts the phone down, opens a drawer and flicks through her Booksearch file. She has no idea what she's looking at – all the authors and titles, customer names and addresses, blur into banners of ink and white space. A woman comes up to pay for a book.

'That's £4.50,' she says. 'I'll put it in a carrier because of the rain.' She has to carry on as normal. The doorbell clatters as the woman leaves and it makes her jump.

The phone rings. What time does she open on Saturday? Does she close for lunch? Nine thirty. No, she's open right through until five. She keeps looking out of the window for David's car.

And at last he opens the door. He must have parked on the road before the shop.

'Where?' he mouths.

She nods towards the back room. 'Wax coat,' she scribbles on a piece of paper.

Then he says out loud, 'Do you mind if I have a look around?'

'No, help yourself,' she says, convinced that they both sound like amateur actors rehearsing a script.

David walks through the shop, stopping once to pick up a book she's got on display above the fireplace. Then he goes into the back room. What's he going to do? Is there anyone else out there? She doesn't think so.

She keeps checking her watch. How can only one minute have passed? It's five minutes before David saunters back.

'Thanks,' he says, as if he's any ordinary customer, and then signals to her that he'll be outside.

It's another ten minutes before the guy comes out of the back room and pops into another aisle – Natural History, Travel. She wants to go and stand next to him, make it obvious that she knows what he's up to, that she's not the fool he thinks she is. But nothing's missing from the Collectable cupboard – she checked when he was out back. It's not him.

He walks up to her desk. 'Nothing today,' he says smiling, standing in front of her, zipping up his coat. 'See you again.'

The bell rings and he's gone.

A bus passes and puddles of rain in the road gush up over the pavement.

Then the bell rings again and he comes back in, followed by David. She doesn't know whose face looks more serious.

'I'm sorry, but we think you might have taken some books without paying for them,' David says. His voice is lower than usual and she knows it's because he's keeping his anger under control. 'We're going to have to ask you…'

'It's okay,' the guy says. His voice isn't the chatty let-me-tell-you-about-my-plans voice she's been used to, and his face looks crumpled as if the threads holding it tight have been cut.

He takes one book out of an outside pocket, a *New Naturalist*, then unzips his coat and takes out another book on beagling from an inside one. Then another one on mountaineering, another on snooker and billiards she knows was published in the thirties because she only put it out on the shelf last week. A Pevsner's *Buildings of England*. And they keep on coming until there are nine of them piled up in front of her.

'How long have you been doing this?' she demands.

'I haven't ...' he mumbles.

'Don't lie to me. How could you come in here and be so friendly to me all this time and do this?'

'Call the police, Breeze,' David says.

'Do you mind if I take this off?' the shoplifter says, tugging at his coat, and he does look hot, all flushed in the face.

'You can bloody well keep it on now,' she says. 'You shit.' She's going to start crying. She fumbles with the phone and forces the tears back down. She's not going to let this bastard see that she's upset. 'I don't know what number...'

'Call on 999. It's okay,' David says and reaches over and puts his hand on top of her open palm on the desk, his fingers touching the cool skin on the inside of her wrist. 'It's over now.'

She's still angry the following day. Yesterday the two police officers had tried to persuade her not to press charges and let them give him a stern warning.

'I'm sure he's learned his lesson,' one of them said.

'But he's been doing it for months, probably longer,' she said.

'You don't have proof of that,' they said. 'And he was very remorseful on the way to the Station, said he wanted to come back and apologise to you.'

'Well he'd hardly say he wanted to come back and steal some more, would he?'

The older one calls in again this morning.

'I know these ex-army boys,' he says. 'And it'll be a waste of time taking this to court. I'm just saying, think about it.'

But she's determined not to give in.

'He's been stealing from me and just because you think it's a load of old books, you don't see it as important. If he'd grabbed £170 from the till, you wouldn't be saying that. Would you?'

He doesn't answer.

'I want to press charges. I don't care that he'll get a minimal fine. You don't know how he's made me feel all this time.'

She turns the 'Closed' sign around after he leaves. She doesn't want to speak to anyone until she feels calmer. She checks her e-mails and immediately thinks of Matthew. And then she feels even angrier, but with herself, for caring about what he might be doing or feeling when he hasn't bothered to get in touch with her and find out how she is. He was the one who walked out on her after promising so much and he can't even manage two fucking words. And the anger feels good. She could phone him, but no, she'll do it by e-mail. It'll be a change from the ones he was used to getting from her. She bangs out a message.

> ...two fucking words, that's all! After all the things you told me, you promised. What the fuck was happening with you? Did you actually mean a single thing you said? I wish I could hate you, then I might feel better...

She doesn't expect him to answer but she feels better for writing it all, is able to concentrate on work, on customers, even forgets about him for the first time when she checks her messages before leaving, opening them without first checking the sender's name. And there he is.

> You're right. I should have. I could have. I am so sorry. I did mean all the things I said at the time I said them... I never intended to hurt you. Please believe me.

Why does she have to be this pleased to hear from him? She's pathetic. But she does feel better, as if someone's loosened metal bands from around her heart. She's missed him so much. She knows she's not being fair to David, but it hurts too much to end it with that last scene in the cottage. If it has to end can't it be with them talking over a glass of wine, like friends?

Seven

She chooses a table near the window so she'll be able to see
him coming. It's raining, the pavement is glossy with puddles, gutters overflowing with water the drains can't take. The
bar is filling with after work drinkers and the air inside is
humid and sweet with damp coats and the smell of wood
burning in the open fire. She nurses her glass of red wine in
both hands. She'd wanted to be as honest as she could and
this time she told David she was meeting Matthew, remind-
ing him of the book-dealer she met in the summer. She had
this first edition of Eric Gill's *Nudes* he'd probably be interested in and he was going to be in the area, so it made sense
to meet up for an hour rather than drive all the way to the
coast on her day off. She thought she saw a flicker of something on his face, but she couldn't be sure and she couldn't
backtrack now. She'd be home by seven, seven thirty at the
latest.

'Hello.' He's standing beside her. She missed him passing
the window, hadn't noticed him come in. She stands to kiss
him and is so pleased that he smells the same. He shakes off
a long dark coat and drops it on a spare chair as she pours
him a glass of wine. He looks tired. The yellow scarf around

his neck highlights the grey under his eyes. The collar of his checked shirt is worn slightly at one tip.

'How are you?' he says.

'Okay.' She says it brightly, but keeps her hands around her glass. She can't trust them not to tremble.

'I've left home,' he says before he's even sat down properly. 'I'm no good to anyone at the moment. I need some time to sort myself out.' He gives a half smile.

But it doesn't reach his eyes – they're flat like the puddles on the pavement outside. She doesn't know what to say or how she should be feeling. This wasn't supposed to happen. Not what she imagined could happen. Not after how certain he was about going home, getting on with the life he had.

'Where are you living?' She can feel her heart beating, wonders if the pulse is showing in her throat.

He shrugs. 'Moving around a bit.'

She should leave it alone, he obviously doesn't want to talk about it, but this doesn't make sense.

'But you want to go back, don't you? That's what you want, isn't it?' She runs her finger around the rim of her glass, notices a small piece of cork floating on the top of the wine, and dips her finger in to pick it out.

'I want to sort myself out but everything I touch at the moment is a disaster. I can't do anything right.' He shrugs again.

She looks up at him, wonders how far he'll have to travel before he finds his way back. Or maybe this is the beginning of something new. But not in the way they both thought it might be.

'Though,' he leans forward, 'I still desire you.' He makes an 'aaargh' face and smiles.

She smiles and blushes at the same time. God, how easy it is for him to make her feel so wanted. Shouldn't she be angry with him? Shouldn't she yell at him? But she doesn't want to. She doesn't have any emotion in her that could make her jump up from the table, throw the glass vase and its happy orange verbena at him and march out. She's as responsible for this as he is – she could have stopped it at any time, just as he could have, but the familiarity and desire she felt with him convinced her there had to be something missing in the life she already had.

'But I'm so glad you're okay.' He runs a finger over the back of her hand.

Okay? This morning she'd opened up the shop and flicked through Sheppard's to find someone who specialised in Modern Firsts. The book had fallen open on Matthew's entry and she'd had to resort to her cold water and slow breathing routine in the kitchen.

'Yes, I'm okay,' she lies.

'Though I don't expect you ever to forgive me.'

She's thought so much about forgiveness. She'd wanted David to forgive her at first, forgive her for something he didn't even know she'd done. Then she thought she had to forgive herself. But now she doesn't know if it's about forgiveness at all. Maybe it all had to happen for some strange and incomprehensible reason – to wake her up to the value of the life she had started to take for granted. She can't work it out. She's tried and she can't come up with any answers that feel completely right. Could it be as simple and corny and irrational as – she fell in love with him? She watches his finger tracing the grain in the table, then looks up at the place on his neck, just below his ear where the damp hair curls against it. And as if he feels her gaze, he runs his hands through his hair, down the back of his neck.

Love – something to do with it is happening here, at some level. She wants to ask him how he feels now, but what's the point? What will she do with what he says? And the months apart from him have taught her something. She might love him but not in the same way she loves David – a love that's been built up over the years, stacked with what they've done and said and seen together, their desire and irritation, their anger and compromise, the nights and days of ordinary life that add up to so much more. Though just sitting here with him looking at her makes her feel she's in a bright place, and she suddenly realises that that's part of what she's missed so much – seeing him seeing her, how under his gaze she felt so much more than she was. Or maybe it was only different. Different but not better.

They share the bottle of wine. He tells her about his latest big auction buy – an eighteenth century Dutch natural history book. 'The best book I've ever had,' he says. '*Merian's Metamorphoses of the Insects of Surinam.* The plates are superb. And it's in its original binding. I'm negotiating a sale at the moment. We should agree on ninety five.'

She automatically thinks £95 but then realises he's talking about ninety five *thousand*. She doesn't sarcastically point out that not everything he's touching is a disaster. She needs to be kind. For her own sake, not just his.

She tells him about hiring someone to work two days in the shop so she can have more time to herself. She doesn't tell him about the plans she and David have made to spend more time with each other, go for the bike rides they used to take, drive up to London for some exhibitions, or even stay at home and sit and read together in the evenings, instead of switching on the television. She doesn't want to expose David to Matthew, or let him know what her life might hold in the future. She doesn't want to feel as if she's carrying Matthew forward with her. The past is safe ground though, just as it always was in their e-mails, and she makes him laugh when she describes being stopped by the police on the slip-road of the motorway for running a red light at the round-about, and how she managed to avoid getting a ticket by in-viting the young policeman to come in out of the rain and sit down.

'I actually lifted my handbag and patted the seat. Hon-estly, I didn't plan to say it. It just sort of... slipped out.'

He lifts his eyebrows and smiles. 'You are a shameful flirt.'

'I'm not,' she protests. Then pauses and says, 'You were very persistent with your seducing, you know.'

'And I was lucky you were so seducible. You were won-derful.'

She smiles but there's something about their exchange that doesn't feel right, as if they're playing the parts of ex-lovers, saying the words they both want to hear.

She takes the Gill book out of her bag to show him, and remembers the shoplifter.

'I caught my shoplifter,' she says. 'He had nine books on him, can you believe that?' And although she feels awkward talking about David, she tells him of the plan they made to trap him.

He smiles. 'You went to a lot of trouble.'

'What would you have done?'

'Claimed on the insurance. Your bookseller's policy cov-ers you for those risks. You did do that for your *House at Pooh Corner* didn't you?'

It had never crossed her mind to do that.

They leave the wine bar and walk together arm in arm to the car park. It's still raining and he pulls her in closer under his umbrella, his hips moving against hers. And again the desire floods through her.

'Let's go this way,' he says, tugging her along the River Walk.

They're the only ones on the path. The noise from the traffic fades and she can hear the water rushing over the weir but knows if she leans over the wall and peers down she won't be able to see anything in the dark.

'I've missed you so much,' he whispers. 'Come here.' And he manoeuvres her against the wall, opening her coat and wrapping his around her. He slides his knee between her legs, gathers her skirt up in one hand and finds her heat.

She's unsurprised at her body's eagerness for him. How easy this all feels. One of them moans quietly.

And again the desire floods through her, and it would be so easy to follow it. But she knows that she can't or she'll be back to how she was in the summer, going over and over each word and touch, imagining and wishing for the next time, breaking herself in two, trying to persuade herself she can deal with the extremes of emotions, waiting and hoping for her love for Matthew to rise like unbaked dough, to prove itself and bake into something hard and real. It still makes her shake with sadness – that this wondrous thing she feels for him can't grow into her life, that it isn't designed to contain the weight and shape of it all. She wanted too much.

Wants and needs. She still wants Matthew at times, but she needs David. She really needs David, the steady pulse of their life. She can't go back. It was too much for her. It would be again.

'There were some things I wanted to know about you,' she says. And he tells her how he folds a newspaper, peels an orange, if he prefers to wake to sun or shadow, exactly the breadth of his chest.

She wanted to know how he moved through life, so she

could fit him into hers. She'd refused to consider what she
would have had to take out, give up, to accomplish this.

'But don't you find it exciting?' he'd said.

'I'm not sure excitement is necessarily a good thing.'

That night she dreams she's on a train, heading north. She
gets off at a station to change trains but she can't see her des-
tination on any notice board. The woman in the ticket office
tells her it's further down the same line and she runs and
runs to get back on her train but it's like running through
water – her legs ache with the hard slow motion – and she's
left her bags on there too and she can see the open doors
and hear a whistle being blown. She's not going to make it.
But she does. And all her bags are safe. She was on the right
train all the time.

Her body floods with relief when she opens her eyes.
And it's not until an hour or so later that she realises Matthew wasn't the first thought in her head when she woke up.

Some days the memory of him creeps over her like cold fog
and voices tell her *he has forgotten you, he never thinks about you
the way you do of him, it's all gone, it meant nothing.* And she reminds herself of one of the quotes she copied from the E.V.
Lucas book – *The art of life is never to think you know what other
people are feeling about you. You are sure to be wrong.* It was real,
she tells herself. It was real for me, and that has to be enough
to know. At those times she still feels she's floating above
her life but then she walks around the house and re-anchors
herself. The things she tried to distance herself from in the
summer are now the things that keep her there. She wants to
hold them all inside her – the grain in the wood-panelling in
the bedroom that reminds her of fish-eyes, the way the
morning light throws pastel colours on the walls, the kitchen

table, the brass rods on the stairs. She wants to swallow them all, make herself heavy with her life again – the rag rug in the kitchen, the skirting boards that took her hours to paint, lying down on the stone floor and cutting in to the wall, the dust and cobwebs in the corners she doesn't clear away often enough, those too. All the parts she nearly gave away, nearly lost, the weight of them securing her, like the weight of David's hand on her head as she falls asleep.

Jon and Katie come for lunch. They've been away for six weeks in Australia. She's so glad to see them, another part of her life that attaches her to the world. She's roasted chickens and vegetables, made a strawberry shortcake gateau – she wants, needs them all to enjoy themselves together today.

'So, tell us all about it.' David pours everyone a glass of champagne.

'We will, but first we've got some other news.' Jon smiles at Katie. 'We're pregnant,' he says. Then they both look at her. 'How do you feel about sleeping with a granddad?' Jon laughs.

'Wow…' David's rubbing his hands through his hair. 'I can't believe…' And then he's up out of his chair kissing Katie and hugging Jon, before coming over to her and kissing her too. 'This is fantastic, isn't it?'

'It is. Congratulations. I'm really pleased for you both.' And she is, she can feel herself beaming. 'So when?' she leans towards Katie – who looks like the least pregnant person in the room – her slim tanned body with its pierced navel, long legs curled up under her, but with a smile that she can't stop from lighting up her face.

'Next summer,' she says. 'End of July.'

'Good,' she says. 'That is so good.'

One more thing has added itself to her life.

'You really never regret not having kids?' David asks her in bed that night. He's cuddling her from behind, his arms wrapped around her, holding her hands close into her body.

'No, really.' Though she did have a little pang of what, jealousy? regret? this afternoon with all the baby talk and future plans spinning around the table. She tells him.

'We still could you know, if you really wanted to. You're not too old.'

'Thanks!' She elbows him lightly. But she really doesn't, never has. It has always been so clear in her mind how her life would have to change to accommodate children, and she doesn't want that. She likes her life as it is. She stops at that thought.

'I like my life as it is,' she says aloud. 'I like our life as it is.' She sees the words sit above their heads in the dark – solid, real. Like the years they have lived and worked through that have brought them both to the same place.

'I'm glad about that,' he says. 'Because so do I.'

They were in Malta on holiday a few years ago. They'd caught the ferry to Gozo. David had been taking pictures of her against a background of yellow sandstone caves at the edge of the cliff when she slipped on the smooth rock, fell flat on her back and started to slide down towards the sea. He dropped the camera, stretched out on his stomach over the lip of rock, grabbed her by the shoulders and pulled her to safety. Coming back on the ferry they both laughed about it – her prancing about for the photo, his camera and clothes covered in algae, the both of them aching from slipping and stretching.

'Somehow I think I'll always end up saving your life, one way or another,' he said.

She touches David more these days. When she folds herself into his arms, or holds her palm up against his to compare the length of their fingers and joke about his little finger being bigger than her thumb, she tries to feel what it is she's really feeling in her body, and watches any thoughts of Matthew scatter through her mind, refusing to let them drag her off on one of many pointless paths. And there's a silence and a stillness in her that she's so grateful for. It makes her consider that real desire is a deep place, that most of the time she's unaware of, but is there the moment she looks for it, reaches out for it.

This morning, when she kisses David as she leaves for the shop, he holds her and rubs the small of her back because she has period pains.

'Take it easy today, Breeze,' he says. 'Okay?'

'Okay.'

As she drives through the lanes, tears well in her eyes, not because she feels sad but because she feels so lucky. Is that selfish? Probably. She still feels guilty too, and sometimes drained by the seep of sadness when thoughts of Matthew tug at her – his words, his smile the second time they met, his hands against her skin. Maybe they might be able to meet up sometime, be friends even. Maybe they could stay in touch, occasionally, if she e-mailed him to say hello. It's stupid isn't it, how two people who said they cared so deeply shouldn't keep a trace of that? It still feels like so much lost. Stop it, she says out loud. Keep your mind on what you're doing, where you are now. Good. Good. And each time she pulls herself back to the present, she hopes she's a little further away from being lost in the full drift.

Minutes after she's put the lights on and she's in the

kitchen making a coffee, she hears the door open with a crash. It's Big Ray who wants to look for a book. His trousers are still an inch above the rim of his shoes, his fawn raincoat belted too tightly. His carer sits in the chair by the desk and reads his copy of the Daily Mail. After about twenty minutes of marching around the shop and the sound of half a dozen books clumping to the floor he comes out of the first aisle clutching a thick quarto size *Castles of Great Britain*. It's a cheap chain-store edition but still a good book. She has it marked at £5.

'Just give me £4,' she says as she slips it in a carrier bag for him.

Then he tells her the same story he's told her more than a dozen times before, will probably continue telling her for as long as he carries on coming in – how a man in a bookshop in another town tried to charge him £10 for a book that was only marked at £1.

'That's wrong,' she tells him again.

'I like it in here, I do,' he says as he leaves.